THE BOSS'S SECRET

A ONE NIGHT STAND AGE GAP AFFAIR

KISMET KAYE

Chapter 1

BRENDA

"What would you like, sweetheart?" The friendly bartender asked me over the throb of the music. They were sporting a lapel pin, bearing their pronouns, and it made me smile.

I was about to answer them when I looked at my phone and sighed. Luke had sent me yet another threatening message. "I don't care what you think. You can run, but I'm going to find you. You and I are going to be together. You can't escape me. I own you."

I looked at the message, shook my head in frustration, and told the bartender, "Get me the strongest thing you have on the bar."

They nodded and said, "Coming right up, darling."

I downed the fourth shot of tequila like a pro. No, I was not a pro, but considering that I had moved across states to be away from my toxic ex, who was sending me threatening messages and telling me he would find me, by any means necessary, I was drinking tequila to steady my mind.

"Would you like me to call you a taxi?" they empathized.

"No, darling, I'm just fine," I tried to reassure us both.

"Well, love, you're in a gay bar, not a straight bar; you don't have to worry. We're gonna take good care of you," they said. Then added quickly, "I'm gonna watch over you like a hawk, baby girl. You seem as if you've had a tough one."

Now, I was self-consciously crying in spite of the loud music and exuberance of my surroundings. Of course, I had a tough month. I had to leave my job, friends, family, and everything I knew because I needed to escape from the first man I had ever fallen in love with. No, I wasn't okay. The bartender moved around and gathered me in her arms. "It's okay, now. This is a safe space. Cry all you want, but you're no longer drinking, you hear me?"

I nodded and hugged them tighter. When I had my fill, I said, "Thank you for your compassion. I wanna pee though. Where do I go?"

They pointed at the hallway. "Girlies go there; boys go there. People who don't care for gender labels go there."

I looked straight at the genderless bathroom and made my way there. Once I was done, I stood looking at the hot mess that I saw in the mirror when the most gorgeous, best-smelling, middle-aged woman I had ever met walked past me into the restroom. She came out, seeing me try to clean the mascara off my face with a paper towel, and offered me a wet wipe from her bag.

"There you go; this should help," she offered, walking out. After cleaning my face and feeling a little sobered up, I went into the hubbub of the club to find her so that I could thank her for her kindness.

I saw her slowly dancing alone to the music, and for the first time, I felt an attraction. I suddenly didn't want to just show her gratitude. I wanted to dance with her.

I walked slowly to her and took her hands. She was startled at first. Then she relaxed, and we started dancing. We moved closer to each other and closer again, until her hands began to rub my back in the warmest, most sensual way. The music and crowd seemed to fade slightly into the background as she filled my senses.

My mind was hazy. I really didn't know what I was doing with this gorgeous woman. I did know what I was feeling, and I knew I wanted to keep feeling more of it.

"Wanna get out of here?" I asked with uncharacteristic spontaneity. She nodded and pulled me to the garage, where her car was parked. We got in, and she drove me to Casa Cipriana. I had heard about this hotel, but I had never been there.

"What would you like?" she asked as soon as we settled into the room.

"I dunno. It's my first time doing something like this; surprise me," I said.

She chuckled and said, "Bold." Then she threw me on the bed.

I lay there and watched her undress. I had never been attracted to women in my life, but she was absolutely gorgeous. She had the perfect body, and I suddenly felt self-conscious about undressing myself as I had some places that I didn't want to show off.

After she undressed, she leaned down and pulled off my pants. Then she whispered, "Shut your eyes."

I asked her why, and she smiled, "You will do it voluntarily anyway when I start. So, do it already."

I asked her why again, and she explained, "Because it's more intense when your eyes are closed. You won't know what I'm going to do."

So, I shut my eyes, and then I felt her take off my panties. At first, I wanted to shut my thighs, but she asked me, "Are you comfortable?"

I said yes because, honestly, somehow I was. She made me feel very comfortable in my exposed state, and that was something that Luke never did. He behaved as if he owned my body. He never gave me a choice or asked any questions, just took what he wanted any time he wanted it. I hadn't really known anything different.

My eyes were still closed when I felt an icy sensation right on my warmest part. The feeling was confusing, something between shock and extreme pleasure. I gasped, and my eyes flew open. She chuckled.

"It's ok. It's ice," she simpered. "Relax."

Then I felt her warm, soft, wet mouth where the ice had been. She gave a little suckle, and before I realized it, a moan had escaped my lips.

***

It was morning. I was exhausted and hungover, but I felt really good. The night may have blurred, but I had felt pleasure in ways I never even thought possible. I looked around the room and found that I was alone. The mystery woman was gone.

On the side table was a breakfast tray, on which there was green juice in a bottle, a pill, and a note.

The note said, "You were knocked out pretty good last night. The green bottle and Advil are for the hangover you'll have, the food is for your hunger, and the envelope…" I looked at the tray and found that there was indeed an envelope. I continued reading the note, "…is for your cab back home. I would have left you a chauffeur, but I needed to get to work early after last night. Hope to see you again. D."

D? D? What began with D? Desiree? Denise? D?

I fell back down, stretching out on the bed. My mind traveled to the events that led me here, which had occurred long before I entered that bar.

I had just gathered enough courage to end my relationship with Luke, my abusive ex-boyfriend. I had to run away from home to a new city to start over if I were ever going to completely escape him. I remembered how the conversation had gone, because it was probably the boldest thing that I had ever done in my life.

"Yes!" I said to Luke when he asked me if this was really what I wanted. Luke had developed the habit of asking me, "Is this really what you want?" every time I said I wanted to leave. It was a manipulation tactic to keep me chained to him.

He wanted me to say, "No," or "I don't know," so that I would remain in the relationship. But I had come to realize that every day I stayed in that toxic relationship, I felt as if I were in the middle of the churning Atlantic Ocean, and I was drowning, only I could not die.

I remembered in a vampire novel I had once read that whenever they wanted to punish a vampire, they would lock him in a coffin and toss the coffin into the ocean. Every time he died, he would wake up again because he was immortal. That was how being in a relationship with Luke made me feel. I couldn't get relief by death. I couldn't get it by life—I was just drowning day after day.

He cheated every single chance he got. In fact, I would walk into clubs, and random girls would walk up to me and ask, "Are you Luke's girlfriend?"

Once, in the club, I even saw a girl wearing a top I thought was missing. That top wasn't just any kind of top. My mother had gotten some limited-edition silk material that was made in just one pattern. She had it because she had met this really wonderful woman who made silk in Italy.

She had told the silk maker that she wanted a design nobody else had, and the woman obliged. She made her dress out of the fabric and then gave me what was left. I handed it to a fashion designer friend of mine who made it into an adorable crop top for me.

I was incredibly sad when I found that the top was missing. Then, I walked into a club, and a random girl I didn't know was wearing that top. So, I walked up to her and furiously demanded her, "How did you get that top?"

She said, "Oh, my boyfriend gave it to me."

I asked her, "Who is your boyfriend?"

She said that he was somewhere around. She began to look around, and I saw my boyfriend, Luke, coming out of the restroom. He saw me and froze. I confronted him.

"There are a lot of things you could have done. Why did you have to give her my top, knowing how much it meant to me?"

I walked out of the club, went home, and took a long nap. The following day, Luke was back at the house with breakfast for me. When I told him I didn't want to see him, he stood in front of me, held my face, looked into my eyes, and asked me, "Is that really what you want, Brenda?"

Of course, it was what I wanted, but because he questioned me, I faltered. I was afraid to tell him that yes, I was certain that I really didn't want to be with him, so I said, "I don't know." That gave him some kind of leeway, and he used it, of course.

The following week was spent with him trying to convince me we belonged together. He bought flowers, sent or brought food, and did literally everything to ensure that I was going to stay with him. Everything was good for a month or two, and then the abuse began again. The toxicity, the gaslighting, the narcissism—he continued everything that made me want to leave him. He started all over again, and the really crazy thing about it was that he knew how to take extra chances.

So, I forgave him for this one and learned that he would double down.

Six months later, I decided that I was done. So, I looked at him and asserted, "I will no longer do this with you. I'm done. I'm breaking up with you and leaving the state." Somehow, in the middle of my introspection, I had decided that the only way I would ever be free of Luke was if I left the state altogether. So, I found a new apartment in New York and paid for it with all my savings. It didn't matter that I didn't have a job there. I was just ready to leave. I would find a job when I settled there.

When he realized that I was in fact leaving the state, he knew I was being real this time. So, he did that thing he always did—held my face, looked into my eyes, and asked me, "Brenda, darling, is this really what you want?"

So, I looked him dead in his eyes and defiantly told him, "Yes, I want to leave you, and I *am* leaving you. I've booked my flight already." Then I thought it probably wasn't safe to have even told him that much.

Then he said, "I'm going to fight for our relationship. You're not going anywhere. We have to talk."

He said that he'd be back tonight. He was going to drag me right back into the hole that I was fighting to get out of. So, before he came back, I packed my bags, went to the airport, and sat down there, even though my flight wouldn't depart for another seven hours.

Finally, my flight number was called, and I breathed a sigh of relief when the plane lifted without incident. I had been in New York for two weeks now, applied to a few jobs, and received rejection letters. I decided it was time to go somewhere, hang out, and unwind. I lived in an apartment complex where there were a lot of actors and

entertainers. It wasn't really an ideal place to live. It was the kind of place actors stayed when they had auditions because it was affordable.

The day before yesterday in the evening, I came out of my apartment and told the first neighbor I saw that I needed a safe place to hang out and unwind. "I don't wanna get groped by dirty men while I'm drinking, " I said.

He suggested that I go to a gay bar, which would be a good fit for what I wanted. He mentioned that he had to go there the next day to check out a new guy he was interested in, and I could join him. He warned me not to expect him to babysit as he was going there to flirt. I thanked him and walked back into my apartment.

The next evening, he was at my door, dressed to the nines in a cowboy costume. "Do I need a costume?" I asked.

"No, girl, but you need a better dress," he said with sass and then waltzed into my house, went straight to my wardrobe. After a few unsatisfied grunts, he found something worthy for me. When we were ready, we headed out.

When I got there, I was a little intimidated. Everybody was having so much fun, and nobody even noticed I was there, which I felt was a good thing. It meant that I could blend into the crowd and just enjoy the vibrant personalities. I found the bar and sat down to relax.

***

My phone rang, and I was dragged back to the reality of the morning. Mercifully, it was a follow up call from one of the companies to which I had applied since I moved to this city. The public relations company was offering an auditing internship in their accounting department, and they had moved my application forward. The interview was at 10AM today. I looked at the time; it was already 8:30AM.

Shit! I couldn't make it home and back in time for the interview, and I also couldn't go in this dress. I dashed into and out of the bathroom in fifteen minutes. I grabbed everything I owned, along with a sandwich, the green juice, and the Advil from the breakfast tray, and ran out of the room where D and I had spent that incredible night.

I called a cab and headed to the office. On our way there, we rode past Primark, and I instinctively rechecked the envelope. Thank God I did because the mystery woman had left me enough to buy a few nice things. I bought a pair of pants, a nice shirt, and a pair of cheap dress shoes. I put them on and headed for the interview. Whoever D was, I was grateful for her generosity.

Chapter 2

DIANA

I had so much to do today that I was regretting the night I had. My head hurt from all the loud music, and I was looking for Luna, my friend. I wanted to yell at her for even suggesting the club when she knew I hated loud music and people.

I had a few interviews to do today at the office, and I also had meetings to attend. I was so exhausted that I decided to pick one of the two. The interviews could be held by the office manager, but the meetings could not be attended by anyone else, so I went to my meetings.

By the time I returned from my meetings, I was so exhausted that I just wanted to sleep. However, I was informed that one of the interns we had interviewed today was going to be working closely with me.

"I already have an assistant," I reminded my manager.

"Yes, but this girl has an in-depth knowledge of how things work within our industry," she explained, "and I think she would be very beneficial."

"Well, I can see her tomorrow. Can't I just go home?" I grumbled.

"You can get to know her tomorrow. However, you have to meet and greet her today," my manager insisted.

So, I went into my office, took a shot of whiskey, and sat down, waiting for this intern who was supposed to be good enough to take the place of the assistant with whom I already worked very well.

A few minutes later, I heard the voice of a young girl as she entered my office.

"Good evening, Miss Argon."

"Stick to Diana, please."

"I'm sorry, Ms. Diana."

Without looking up, I said, "Sit down."

"Thank you, ma'am," she said and sat down.

"I'm told you have an understanding of the PR industry. Is that true?" I asked.

"I don't have as in-depth an understanding as you do, but I have a basic understanding. I studied communications at the university, and I have worked for a while as a junior PR consultant."

"That's impressive," I said, looking up. "Where did you wor…"

Before she could answer, I saw her face and froze.

"I moved here from Chicago," she said.

"Uh, umm, why did you move?" I asked, stammering like a novice.

"Well, it's a long, complicated story,"

"What's the shorter version?" I asked, curious.

"Well, I just needed a fresh start. A lot happened back at home," she said.

"Okay, you can begin tomorrow, and I'll brief you on everything you need to know then," I said.

"Thank you very much, ma'am, for this opportunity. I will not disappoint you," she said.

Not until she got to the door did I realize that I had not asked for her name. Embarrassed, I inquired, "What is your name?"

She turned, smiled, and said, "Brenda, Brenda Jenkins."

"Okay, Miss Jenkins, see you tomorrow, and please be early. I have meetings to get to. While I already have an assistant, we'll be promoting her to an administrative position before the end of next week. You'll have to shadow her to learn how to work with me. I need you to think quickly on your feet. Is that something you can do?"

"Yes, ma'am, I can definitely do that," she replied. I nodded in acknowledgement, and she walked out of the door.

***

As soon as she left, I grabbed the bottle of whiskey and drank directly from it. What the fuck was going on? I immediately called Luna on the phone.

"Hi, Luna."

"Hey, what's up?" she said.

"Girl, you got my ass in a crack."

"I'm always getting your ass in trouble, but what specifically was it this time?" she retorted.

"Remember the club you took me to yesterday?" I asked.

"Oh, yes, I remember. You seemed to be having so much fun, and without me," she said.

"Yeah, well, that fun has come back to bite me in the ass."

"What do you mean? Did you ruin your meeting because of your hangover?" she asked.

"I wish that was the case, but it wasn't," I said.

"So, stop holding back, and give me the full story. What is going on?" she nudged.

"You know how I was dancing with a hot girl last night, and then I ended up leaving with her?"

"Oh yes, I saw you with that hottie, but I was wondering if she wasn't too young for you," she teased.

"Well, two things. One, I did leave with her, went to the hotel, and things got even steamier. Two, she's definitely too young for me. And three, I just saw her again."

I confided, "You know, I wasn't too mad at you this morning for making me go to that loud party last night because I had a beautiful experience with that young woman. She was drunk, so I doubted that she was going to remember much of it. But, as I sat down, looking at that same young woman in my office, hoping that she didn't remember, I 'blessed' you yet again."

"That's about four, maybe even five, things you just said, not two," she bantered. I chuckled, and then she inquired, "Wait…Where did you see her?"

"Well, remember that my company was having a few interviews, and I asked you if you knew anyone who would be interested?"

"Yeah, I didn't have anyone that I thought would be able to do the job. You know, being polite, let's just say that working with you isn't the easiest thing, and people need to be able to think on their feet," she said.

"Well, one of the interns who came in today was—"

"Oh, no," she gasped, cutting me short. That was one of the things I liked about Luna. I didn't have to explain much. She usually got it.

"Well, I thought the plan was to go there and drink. It was never to hook up with someone. There are certainly a few things for which you're allowed to blame me. This isn't one of them. Considering the fact that you've been, well, a little too uptight of lat, even though I'm really happy that you got laid, I am not responsible for your choice. I will say I did think that not having sex was probably wh…"

"Luna!" I yelled, cutting her short.

"Yes, ma'am?" she said, coyly.

"Focus on the issue that I have at hand."

"What? What is the problem? You don't have to interview her, nor do you have to hire her," she said.

"You see, that's the problem. Since I was at the party last night, I was too tired to handle both sets of engagements today. So, I went to my meetings and had my office manager handle the interviews. She hired this girl, and now this girl will be working closely with me as my assistant. My current assistant is getting promoted, so now I have to work in close relations with *a girl I slept with* after the party last night. And not just *any* girl, a *much younger girl* who currently has to look up to me as *a mentor and a boss.*" I kicked myself.

"What did she say?" Luna asked me.

"She didn't say much. I still don't know if she remembered me. She was pretty drunk last night."

"This is all so much," she said.

"Tell me about it. I'm going home to drink, sleep, and figure out how to start tomorrow with this girl. Bye, Troublemaker."

"I'm so sorry you're dealing with all of this," she consoled.

I hung up the phone, packed up, and started heading home.

On my way to exit the building, I saw that it was raining, and Brenda was standing and staring out of the office windows. After contemplating ten times in my head whether or not I should walk up to her, I finally did.

"Miss Jenkins, why are you still standing here?" I asked.

"Well, I have to walk to the bus station because I'm saving my money, but it's raining. I can't walk in that rain, so I'm just going to wait here till it stops," she explained.

"Where do you live?"

"Lower Manhattan," she said.

"Well, I live in Soho. Get in the car; I'll drop you."

As soon as she entered the car, I turned on some music so that the tension between us, which I was not sure she realized existed, would be doused. As the music came on, she wiggled her nose slightly and said, "It's weird, but I can remember smells."

"What do you mean?"

"Something about this car and your perfume smells very familiar. I'm trying to rack my brain as to when and where I found that smell."

"Maybe you smelled it somewhere else," I immediately steered us away from the conversation.

Her phone rang, and I was thankful. She brought out her phone to answer the call, and the envelope I had used to leave money for her this morning fell out of her bag. She picked up the envelope immediately, and then something caught her eye. She looked on my dashboard and found the same kind of envelope there.

I *might* be a *little* compulsive about a few things. For example, I used the same kind of envelopes for every correspondence because I wanted others to remember me when they saw that envelope. It was a business branding strategy.

Right there and then, I realized that I was stupid last night to have used that envelope, knowing fully well that anyone who had it could recognize me. After all, my initials were on the envelope. It served its purpose too well this time. She looked at me and said, "*D* is for *Diana?*"

I stopped the car and said, "Believe me, I didn't know that you were coming to my office today."

"What would you have done if you knew?"

"Not hired you."

"I was the best intern among every other person who applied," she said confidently.

"Well, the manager highly recommended you, but when I saw you, I was a little taken aback. When I thought that you didn't remember who I was, I found some respite. And now that you do, things are a little awkward. I'm going to be your boss and your mentor, and I don't know how to navigate this relationship," I confessed.

"It's not a relationship," she said, smiling. "Don't bother your head about it. I promise that it's not a big deal."

I took a deep sigh and said, "You sound very comforting, but that's not how I am. I overthink things."

"Well, Miss Diana, let this be the one thing you don't overthink."

I was looking at her; she sounded like someone who had been through a lot in life. So, I asked, "What really brought you to New York?"

"Well, I guess you've earned the answer to that question," she said. "I had a very abusive boyfriend who seemed as if he was going to chase me to the ends of the Earth to keep me bound to him. The only way that I would have gotten away from him was by leaving the state, so I left."

"Couldn't you have just gotten a restraining order?"

"He didn't commit any crime. He was emotionally and verbally abusive. None of that results in jail time. Besides, if I were going to ask for a restraining order, I had to have proof of threat to life, and I didn't have any. I also knew that if I let him remain in my life, he would not have set me free. He was going to drive me to the brink of destruction, so I had to leave," she explained.

Brenda smiled and told me, "If you remain stopped here on this street, we're never going to get to our destination. So, I think we need to get going now."

When we got to downtown Manhattan, she said, "I would like to be dropped off here. I'll find my way home."

"Nonsense. I'll drop you at home. Where is your house?" I insisted.

"It's nothing fancy, and I don't think I want you to see it. Just drop me here; I'll go home," she insisted. "You've been so kind to me."

"Are you sure you'll be okay?"

"Yes, I'll be fine. Also, thank you for these clothes, by the way."

"What do you mean?"

"Well, when I woke up in the hotel hungover, I hate to admit that I had completely forgotten that I had an interview today. When I received the confirmation call, I realized that I could not go home if I was to be on time for the interview, and I had nothing to wear. When I opened that envelope you left me, I saw that you generously included money to take me home and buy me nice things. So, I went into the nearest Primark store and bought myself clothes that I could wear for today's interview. I haven't been home yet today."

"Now I really have to drop you at home as I should have, and would have, done this morning if my timing had been better," I insisted.

"You never really take 'no' for an answer, do you?"

"Sometimes I do; sometimes I don't. Let's consider this one of the latter times," I said.

"Fine, I live at an apartment complex for actors trying to break into Broadway," she said.

"Is it all the way down?"

She nodded her head and said, "That's why I asked you to drop me here. I was going to find my way home."

"Again, nonsense. I'll drop you off at home; I insist."

I started the car and began to drive. It wasn't so awkward anymore, but neither of us were saying anything. When we got to her apartment complex, she looked at me and said, "Thank you very much, ma'am. I'll see you at work tomorrow." Then, she got out of the car and went in without even looking back.

I started my car and drove with a speed that confused even me. When I eventually screeched to a halt at an intersection, I asked myself what I was running from. When I could not answer my personal rhetorical question, I started driving like a sane person again. *Ridiculous.*

When I got home, I had some more whiskey, made myself dinner, took a shower, and climbed into my bed. But, sleep didn't come. Instead, I kept imagining her body, her hands on my body, and how it felt to make love to her last night. Going to the bar and having one or two no-strings-attached encounters was not new to me. In fact, not dealing with the work of relationships, just seemed easier. Something about this girl was different though. She made my body feel so good. I had not felt like this in a long time. Whatever it was, I was going to figure it out. For now, all I wanted to do was sleep. I imagined that she was lying down beside me. I went to bed hoping that by tomorrow, all of this delusion and infatuation would have faded, and I'd be able to concentrate and work professionally with Miss Brenda Jenkins.

Chapter 3

BRENDA

I woke up again this morning to a bunch of threatening messages from Luke. I needed to have my number changed very soon because there was no way I was going to let this old baggage weigh me down in my new life. I needed to focus, and right now, he was messing with my ability to concentrate. I had given him enough of my life. I would not willingly give him a second more.

I had a bigger issue on my mind. How in the world was I going to work with Miss Diana? I could not extricate her from my thoughts all night, and they were definitely not appropriate thoughts to have about one's boss. I enjoyed the memory of all the things she did to me in that hotel room. She may not have remembered my face, but I remembered how my body felt and how it reacted to her. My mind and body craved more of her.

A part of me was apprehensive about work today, but another part of me was a little too excited to see her. I took out every single thing in my closet, trying to figure out what to wear. When I couldn't make a decision and was running out of time, I went downstairs and knocked on the door of my new friend.

"Hey, newbie," he said with a broad smile as soon as he opened the door.

"Hello," I said to him.

"What do you need?" he said with pretended testiness.

I wondered why this guy was so sassy. Couldn't he muster politeness?

"Well, I have a long story to tell you, but I'm going to make it short because I don't have time, and I have to get to work," I said.

"Well, make it snappy, girl. I have to go finish my mimosas," he said with a wave of his manicured hand.

"Well, after the party you took me to, I hooked up with a woman," I admitted.

"Wait, aren't you straight?" he said mockingly.

"Well, I am, or, at least, I was," I said with a grimace.

"So, what is this problem? Did the woman ask you out for a date?" he said.

"Oh, it's more complicated than that," I said.

"What's the complication, child? I need to get back to what I'm doing. Be fast," he said.

"Well, I sort of unknowingly applied for and got a job at the company where she works. I will be her assistant. Now I have to go to work, but I don't know what to wear. I don't want to give her any ideas, but I also don't want to look stupid to her. Every single thing I have, I think it's stupid. So, could you please help me?" I urged.

"Ooh, that is complex," he agreed.

"I know, I know. It's complex. That's why I need your help," I pleaded.

"Fine, let's just go upstairs and see what in your wardrobe says 'not thirsty but still hot,'" he said. Honestly, it was the correct description for what I wanted to wear.

So, I trudged behind him like a teenager following her mother in a store, until we got to my wardrobe. When we got there, I did the same thing, throwing my things around until he found something that he thought was worthy.

"Let me get this straight," he asked, "You have a crush on her?"

"No," I said.

"But you're worried about how you would look in front of her?"

"Yes," I said.

"Hmmm, did you like the sex?" he asked again.

I was taken aback by that question, but he was serious.

"Best I ever had," I admitted with a smile that I could not suppress.

"How did you feel when you recognized her again?" he asked.

"I dunno, shy?"

"Shy… hmmm. Why?"

"Look, I have never been with a woman before. As a matter of fact, I consider myself very straight," I said. He laughed out loud.

When I was done dressing, he pulled me to the mirror and said, "Baby, I have been gay since I could say 'dada,' and I can smell all the queerness you're trying to push down. Anyway, here is some pink lip gloss for luck," and then he pulled out a fruity lip gloss from his pocket and handed it to me.

"Do you always carry lip gloss in your pocket?" I asked.

"Oh, no, I only carried it today because I have seen you before today. I know that you're clearly bad at a lot of things, 'girl,' so I'm helping out." He made air quotes with his hands. "Now put it on, and stop questioning your Fairy God Unctie, Cinderella," he said.

"What is your name? I'm realizing that I have not asked until now," I said.

"My name is Paxton, but you can call me Paxie, or Fairy God Unctie," he said with much flair.

I laughed and said, "Okay, Unctie."

"Play it cool, Chile, and I wanna hear all of the beautiful details when you return from work."

I got out of the house and headed to the office. When I got there, Diana wasn't there yet, so I just sat down in the lobby to wait for her. She came in a few minutes later with her assistant– a short, bubbly girl with long blonde hair and really curly lashes. I had no idea why I was noticing the assistant like that, but for some reason, I started looking at her to see if I was up to par. As soon as Diana saw me, she smiled sweetly and said, "Allison, meet Brenda. You'll be training her to take over your tasks. Brenda, this is Allison, my assistant, and the person who you'll learn from before she moves over to management."

I nodded and walked behind them, watching as the assistant rescheduled Diana's day, curated her social media posts, and filtered out clients from the random messages she got in her inbox. I also overheard them talking about random things like Diana's relationships and plenty of women sliding into her DMs, expressing their interest in being with her.

For some reason I can't explain, the attention that Diana was getting made me feel jealous. At some point, Allison asked Diana if she had been with anyone recently. I felt really flustered, and I looked away. Diana coughed and told her, "Well, that is above your pay grade, Allison."

"Oh, you've been with someone?" Allison said excitedly. "Tell me, who was she?"

"You have too many questions this morning, Allison. Go and train the person I asked you to train and let me be," Diana replied.

Not getting the message, Allison persisted, "Surely, you're going to have to tell me who it is." Then she looked at me and said, "Come on, Brenda, let's go survey the office."

As we got to the door, I looked behind me, and Diana was right back on her laptop. Maybe she truly had moved on. I told myself that I should feel relieved. If she wasn't making an issue out of this, I didn't see why I should either. Maybe I should move on too.

I focused on work the entire day, following Allison around and having her show me the ropes. When the day was over, I went down to the cafeteria to see if I could get some cheap leftover lunch. Usually, whatever was left in the cafeteria at office complexes would be sold cheaper. At least that was how things ran in the company I formerly worked for in Chicago.

When I got down there, I met a nice lady, and I asked her, "Do we have any cheap leftovers that I can buy and take back home?"

She looked at me funny for a while and then asked me, "What did you say?"

I repeated myself.

"Do you work at the Uptown Agency?" she asked.

I replied, "Yes."

"Oh, darling, you get lunch free," she said.

"Oh, really?" I replied.

"Of course," she said.

"I missed lunch. Is there anything else I can have?" I asked.

"Come on. Here, I'll pack up something nice for you," she said.

I waited as she packed up a plate of tater tots and rice for me, throwing in some pieces of grilled chicken, vegetables, and a big plate of salad. I was really happy because I had been scrimping on coupon meals for the last two weeks. I had overshot my spending budget, and I had literally nothing left.

On my way out of the cafeteria, I ran into Diana. She was on a business call. When she saw me, she beckoned for me to wait. I stood there, shifting from one foot to the other, while Diana finished her call. As soon as she was done, she looked at my hands and asked, "What is that?"

"Oh, I just stopped by the cafeteria to get some meals I could take home," I said.

"You didn't have lunch?" she asked.

"Oh, I was so busy that I didn't have lunch," I said. That was a lie. The truth was that I didn't have lunch because I thought it was something I had to buy, and if I used all the money I had with me for lunch, I wouldn't have any left for dinner. So, I decided to wait and buy the leftovers cheaper so that I could save it for lunch and breakfast tomorrow.

Diana looked at me and said, "I have a feeling that you're lying to me, but I'm in no mood to argue. Come, we're going to have dinner," she said.

"I don't think that's a good idea," I said immediately.

"What do you mean it's not a good idea?" she asked.

"Well, we work together and all," I said.

"People who work together have dinners together, Brenda. Besides, you're about to become my assistant, and we're going to be working closely together. I should inform you that it will involve a lot of lunches and dinners on my account. Get used to it, and get in the car," she said.

I smiled. She smiled too, and then Diana asked me, "You like free food that much?"

"That was not why I was smiling," I said.

"So why were you smiling?" she asked me as soon as I got in the car.

"You're very authoritative," I said, and then for some reason, I added, "not just in the office."

She screeched to a halt, looked at me, and said, "Brenda!"

"Whoops," I said, apologetically.

She chuckled and said, "I don't need you to apologize. But, I must warn you, if you keep saying things like that around me, it'll be very hard to work together."

"It won't happen again," I said.

Then she laughed and said, "Gosh, I have so much to teach you."

We finally arrived at a very fancy restaurant, and we went in. I didn't know half of the names on the menu, so she asked, "Would you like me to pick what you eat?"

"Please, help me out," I said.

She chuckled and picked something called "deviled pasta." The name alone made me nervous, but when the food came, I realized it was just deviled eggs that were carved out from inside and replaced with pasta salad.

"It is my very strong opinion that we should defund bourgeois restaurants," I said.

"Why? What do you have against a good life?" she said.

"Oh, nothing. Just that their names are so complicated, and their foods are so expensive," I said.

"Nothing on this menu is expensive," she said.

"I haven't Googled you yet, but I feel like if I did, I'd find you on the Forbes list," I said.

She laughed and said, "Forbes list is such a stretch, and you're so dramatic."

"Well, a little drama is good for the world, don't you think?" I said.

"I'll take your word on that one," she said. "Now eat your food and tell me the real reason why you were going to scavenge the lunch lady's trays after work."

"You have to promise that you will not try to do anything about it," I said.

"That's a hard promise for me to make. Fine, I won't try to do anything about it. What's the problem?" she said.

I told her about my financial situation and immediately added, "But I work now, so I can easily cover my groceries. I just have to wait for the next paycheck. Until then, please let me collect food from the lunch lady at the end of work, and stop trying to buy me food."

"Fair enough," she said. "You can always eat lunch and still go back to the lunch lady at the end of the day, you know that, right?"

"Yes, that is something I intend to do," I told her.

"Good. Take advantage of the resources that are at your disposal, okay?"

"Yes, ma'am," I said.

She stared right into my eyes, and I could swear that I could see all the secrets of the world resting behind her sultry eyes. And then she said, "This is difficult for me."

"What's difficult for you?" I asked.

"I'm looking at you right now, Brenda, and all I want to do is flip you on the bed and take off your clothes, like the first time," she said.

I could feel my insides burn, and it was a good burn.

"I don't know what to say," I said.

"You don't have to say anything, actually," she said. "I just needed to get that out of the way. What happened between us the first time, regardless of how inappropriate it seems right now, I really want it to happen again," she said.

Before I could stop myself, I said, "Me too."

The rest of the dinner went by silently, with the occasional brush of hands. The ride home was even worse. Every time she leaned over to make a turn, I wanted to grab her face and kiss her.

As soon as she dropped me off at home, I ran straight to my door. I didn't even want to look at her because if she had looked into my eyes, she would have seen the wanton lust there. When I walked into the complex, Paxton was waiting for me.

"I just saw a really nice SUV drop your ass off, who was that?" he asked me.

"Diana," I said.

"Wait, thee Diana?" he exclaimed.

"Yes, that one. Can I please go in?" I said.

"Hell no, Chile. You're going to tell me everything," he said.

"Well, can I drop everything in my hand in my fridge before I start telling you a story that I don't think you should know?" I said.

"I have nothing better to do. None of my auditions came through today, so I'm right behind you. Come on, let's go," he said.

We entered my apartment and began to talk, and while we did, my phone buzzed. I looked at it, and it was Luke. He knew I was in New York, and he was here to find me. Dread immediately rose to my face.

"Okay, honey, I know I'm enjoying the story between you and your lady friend at the office, but I think something worse is going on, and I think you need to tell me right now," Paxton said.

I told him all about Luke and how I ran all the way to New York to be far from him. When I was done, Paxton nodded and said, "If that boy ever comes to this complex to find you, he should know that he's going to be leaving here with a broken nose, a broken arm, or broken teeth. Something will break. Don't you dare worry about him," he said.

Chapter 4

DIANA

As I drove away from her apartment complex, I realized that I couldn't take this anymore. So, I drove back to the complex, parked in front of it, contemplated going inside, but then I realized that I couldn't go in because I didn't know which apartment was hers. I sat outside for a few minutes and then decided to call her. I called her twice, but she didn't pick up. Just as I was about to drive away, she called me.

"Hello, ma'am, is there a problem?" she asked.

"Umm, umm, I, I think…" I stuttered.

"What's the problem, ma'am? Is something wrong?" she asked again.

"Well, the only thing wrong is that I feel like I shouldn't have let you go back to your house after dinner. I'm parked outside your apartment complex like an idiot, and I just want you and me to go back home and be with me," I finally managed to say.

She was silent for a really, really long while, well not too long, but it felt like an eternity. When I was tired of waiting for her to say something, I added, "You could always say no, and it will not affect your work or our working relationship. You don't have to keep silent."

Then she said, "Oh, that's not why I was silent. I was just packing a bag."

I looked toward the main door of the apartment complex and saw her standing outside with a small bag. I smiled as soon as I saw her, and she smiled too. She got into the car, dropped her bag, and then pulled my face to hers and kissed me passionately. I was taken aback and looked at her funny.

"I've wanted to do that all evening," she said.

"Me too," I said, and then I pulled her in and kissed her again.

When we got to my apartment, she looked around and said, "Well, you're rich-rich!"

"I can't argue with that," I laughed.

"I really like your house," she said and sat down on the sofa.

"Would you like something to drink?"

"How did you know?"

"You look very nervous, a drink will help you take the edge off," I said.

"Yes, please, I would very much like a drink." She asked, "Did you just start your company?"

"You don't need to make small talk, you know," I said, "because I know that you've researched my company enough to know that I didn't just start it. You can ask me personal questions."

"How did you start your company?"

"Well, my parents used to run a promotion firm, and then when my father died, he said whoever could fix the PR agency part of the firm could run it. My brother didn't see a reason to be caught in a stupid competition with me, so he told my father that he was the one who was well trained to run the company, and if my father wasn't willing to give it to him, he was going to go ahead and start his own.

So, he left and tried to start a company, while I tried to fix this one for my father. I did fix it, so my father changed the name of the company and handed it to me. After my father died, my brother tried to take the company back from me. The board didn't let him, so I'm running it for now."

"Well, I'm done drinking," she said, "What were those plans you said you had for me?" she asked, her tone indicating curiosity and eagerness.

I laughed and said, "Undress."

"Yes, ma'am," she said and took off every single piece of clothing she had on.

When she was done, I said, "Lie down on your back, shut your eyes, and open your legs."

She did as I had asked. The last time I saw her like this, she was too drunk to understand what was happening to her. Right now, I wanted her to feel everything I wanted to do to her,

I looked at her face as I inserted my finger into her. She gasped, opened her eyes, and locked them on mine. It was so hot to watch her be that vulnerable, and then I increased my speed and intensity as she moaned out loud and rocked her hips to match my motion.

When it seemed she could take no more, I planted my mouth on her throbbing sex and began to suck on her. She threw her legs open even wider and started to scream. Good thing my house was soundproofed. She reached the height of pleasure with so much energy that I got scared that she might faint.

I woke up before her and watched as she slept, her face innocent. This was going to be so complicated. I wasn't sure what I was doing, but I was sure that I liked it. I was not one to make a lot of stupid decisions, and I wasn't sure why I was making this one. I also wanted to tell Luna what was going on, but I knew that she was going to tell me to stop because this was going to be bad for my career and my mental health.

She would be right, but this felt so wrong and so good at the same time that I wasn't sure which feeling I should go with. So, I stuck with "good" because it had been such a long time since I felt this way.

Eventually, she opened her eyes and asked me, "Do you always stare at people when they sleep?"

I smiled and said, "Only if they are as beautiful as you are."

"How many beautiful people have you been with? You must have women lined up to be with you."

"To be honest, I haven't been with a lot of people. I lie to my friends that I've been getting laid, but you were the first person in many months," I said.

"Do you say that to all your girls to make them feel special?"

I laughed. "Most women don't do that. I definitely don't," I assured her.

"I'll note it," she said.

I looked at the time. It was 4 a.m., so I told her to get some sleep since we had work tomorrow. At the mention of work, she began thinking aloud how we were going to get to work tomorrow. Before I could say anything, she concluded, "I know, I'll take an Uber while you drive to work."

"That sounds like a very good idea," I said. "You have thought this through, haven't you?"

"Well, I didn't really think it through until you mentioned work right now," she admitted.

"Come on, let's go back to the room," I said. She stood up, followed me, and gasped as soon as she entered my bedroom.

"Well, would you like to go for another round before you go back to sleep?" I asked.

"I thought you'd never ask," she said. She reached out for me, pulled me to her, and then planted a kiss on my throat. I let out a gasp.

"I wanna try something new with you," I said.

"What?"

"Just wait, I'm coming," I said.

I went into my closet and came out with a curved sex toy that could be inserted into the two opposite holes at the same time. She looked nervous, so I said, "We will not try anything that you're not comfortable with."

"No, it's okay. I wanna try whatever this is," she said.

So, I nodded and lubed up the toy. I inserted my fingers into her vagina and worked her up into a frenzy. When she seemed like she was calming down, I inserted both ends into her carefully and slowly, waiting for her gasps to come down before I started the toy.

When I started it, she began to moan quietly. As I increased the intensity of the vibrator, she began to scream louder and louder. I watched as her clit rose and throbbed, seeking attention. I leaned in and planted my tongue on her clit and began to rub and suck feverishly. She thrashed, cried in intense pleasure, and begged for more. Eventually, she reached her peak, and she moaned my name.

I let up and watched as she succumbed to the intensity of the pleasure, and then she whispered hoarsely, "Thank you."

Not sure if she was up for cuddling, I simply laid beside her to sleep, but she rolled into my body and nestled there. I cradled her in my arms like she was a child, and I let her sleep. As she slept, I thought of ways in which this could be described as wrong and decided to not give it a second thought.

"Regrets are for mornings," I said to myself and then planted a kiss on her forehead and went to sleep.

***

I got to the office before her Uber arrived and met Allison waiting for me in the lobby. As soon as Brenda arrived, I greeted her, "Good morning, Ms. Jenkins. Did you have a good night?"

She smiled sweetly and replied, "Yes, ma'am, I did."

"Good," I said, "because we have a lot of meetings today, and I need to be in a good mood for all of them, which is usually not the case."

"No worries, ma'am," Allison reassured.

My meetings began, and she sat with me throughout all of them, exchanging glances with me the entire time. After my last meeting for the day ended, I asked her, "Are you hungry?"

"I thought we agreed that we wouldn't be buying me food."

"Well, this is different. I'm hungry, and I want to go out and eat, and I want to go with you. Stop arguing. Let's go," I insisted.

"Have I told you that I like how authoritative you are?"

"If you say that again, I'm going to find a wall to pin you to," I said.

"What makes you think I have a problem with being pinned to walls?" she asked playfully.

"Are you sure this is your first time being with a woman?" I inquired.

"Yes."

"Well, you're so good at flirting and wondering why," I replied.

"It's simple. I look at you, and I just want to say the weirdest shit that comes into my head."

"Well, I'm glad I have that effect on you," I said.

"Would you want to know the effect you have on me?" she teased.

"Okay, I need to stop right now. I am excessively turned on, and I don't know what to do." I admitted.

"Good, now we're both on the same page."

"What do you mean?" I asked.

"Watching you in the meetings, seeing you take charge like that, and seeing how you asserted yourself when the men tried to condescend got me warm in all the right places. Now that you're feeling the same thing I was feeling, I think we can go have lunch now."

"Let's go back to my office, and get my bag first," I suggested.

"Okay," she agreed. As we walked back to my office, I decided to take a bold step. As soon as I got to my office, I pulled her inside, shut the door, and said, "I would like you to repeat every single thing that you've been saying to me for the past ten minutes."

"I don't have to repeat anything. However, I can do this," she said, leaning in closer.

Then she pulled my skirt up, knelt down below me, and said to me, "You'll have to tell me what feels good, because I am only guessing."

"We don't have time for that."

"You're the boss, Diana. There is nothing we don't have time for; now teach me how you like to be pleasured."

At this point, I thought I was already so heavily pleased that all she had to do was touch me, and I was going to cum. I rested against the wall, and bent my leg onto a chair, giving her a full gaze at my vagina.

"This smells beautiful," she said.

"Thank you," I whispered.

She brought her lips close and kissed me there. I gasped as soon as she did it.

She looked up at me and innocently asked, "Did you like that?"

I nodded, so she did it again, this time, with passion. Then she began sliding her fingers in and out as she licked me.

I began to shake and grab onto anything I could find for stability, and then I began to moan out loud. I didn't know when I grabbed her head and began to grind into her mouth. I didn't care that anyone who walked past that office at that moment could hear me. I just knew that I wanted to fuck her mouth the way that I had never fucked anyone before. Then I began to feel the familiar swell in my lower abdomen.

"I'm cumming," I yelled out. She just pulled me closer and sucked on my clit harder as I ground against her face and then l burst. I was shivering and moaning as I came all over her.

As soon as I was done, I collapsed into the chair, shaking. She stood up from the floor, her face covered in my moistness, and she said, "Wow, that was beautiful to watch." Then she laughed softly.

"I want to eat now."

"Same."

And just as she was about to go into the private bathroom in my office to clean up, someone knocked on the door of my office.

Chapter 5

BRENDA

Ι had never run that fast in my entire life. As soon as I shut the door behind me, I heard Allison coming into the office.

"What are you doing here? I thought you had gone home," Diana asked her.

"Oh, I had, but HR told me that there were some documents you had to sign to approve my promotion," she said.

"You couldn't have brought them tomorrow?" Diana questioned.

"I could have, but I told HR that I would need to go to the doctor tomorrow," she said.

"But what's wrong? Why do you have to go to the doctor?" she asked, concerned.

"Nothing serious. My eyes feel weird, and my boyfriend thinks I might need to see an eye doctor. So,

I'm going to an appointment for my eyes," she explained.

"Alright, drop the things you need me to sign on a table and get the hell out of my office because I need to go home. I'm not going to take a look at those papers until tomorrow," Diana stated firmly.

"Alright, Boss, I hear you," she said, and as she went out the door, Diana said, "Keep me posted on what they say at the doctor, will you?"

"Yes, ma'am," she replied and exited the room. As soon as I heard the door close, I came out of the bathroom, and Diana began to laugh.

"We can't keep sneaking around like this," I said.

"What do you have against sneaking around?"

"For starters, we're not children," I said.

She started laughing, and for a minute, I couldn't understand why she was laughing. Then I caught onto the irony. She was way older than I, and here *I* was telling *her* that we were not children. Suddenly, I began to laugh too.

"Come on, old lady, let's go have dinner. We can discuss what children should and should not do when we get home," she suggested.

"Home?"

"Yes, home. We're going back to mine," she said.

"I have a house, you know."

"oh, I know you have a house. I'm going to go there, and you're going to pick a few things. We've got to go back to my house," she said.

For some reason, I was taken aback, so I looked at her and said, "I hope you didn't think that I'm a freeloader."

"What do you mean by freeloading?" she inquired.

"I mean that you have all this money and this nice house, and then you literally pay my salary. I don't want to feel like I'm taking things from you because you have them to give me," I explained.

"Okay, you need to learn how to stop being insecure about the things that I offered you," she said.

"There are other interns in your office," I said, "and they don't get free Uber rides to work, free lunches and dinners, or access to the boss's house."

"Well, Boss didn't meet them at a bar, hook up with them, and fall for them," she said, and suddenly she caught herself.

I wanted to ask her what she meant by "fall for me," but I saw that she caught herself immediately, so I decided to let it go and walked outside the office instead.

"I didn't mean to say that," she said when we got into the car.

"What did you mean to say?"

"I didn't mean to say that I had fallen for you," she confessed.

"Why did you not mean to say that?"

"Well, because it might just complicate things for you. I see how hard this whole thing is for you already. You won't even have lunch with me without second-guessing yourself and asking a bunch of questions."

"Well, it doesn't mean you shouldn't be honest about your feelings," I said.

"Well, I don't know what to say, especially given the fact that we're not sure if you're a lesbian or not."

"I understand why that might be a problem," I said, "but this is all new for me. I'm trying to understand what this might mean for my sexuality and my future."

"I get that, and I don't want to push you, which is why I'm sorry for bringing up my feelings like that.

"I think I should stay in my own house tonight," I said.

"Not a problem," she said, and then we drove to my apartment in silence.

Before I exited the car, I looked at her and said, "You should never be sorry for saying how you feel. Yes, this is all new for me, and I'm trying to figure it out. You're an amazing woman, and I love spending time with you. I believe that things will become clear in the future. Until then, please don't expect me to give you what you want from me at the moment."

She nodded and answered, "See you tomorrow." Then she drove off.

***

"Well, I kind of understand why you told her that," Paxie said when I told him later.

"You do?" I asked him.

"Yes, I do. I understand. However, I also say this from the other side. There's always a danger of falling in love with a straight person," he said.

"Hold up; don't go too far," I said, "falling in love? When did we get there? Please, don't make my heart beat faster than it already is. I already feel like I'm going to die of anxiety having to work closely with her tomorrow. I know that she has feelings for me. No, please don't say words like 'love' yet. They are such a big deal, and you can't just throw them around, especially in my kind of dynamic."

"Well, your dynamic is really weird," he said, and then added, "I don't really know how you intend to fix this, but I'm a little worried about you. I hope you're making all the right decisions, baby girl."

I nodded and laid down to sleep.

"Well, that is my cue to go to my room and prepare for my audition tomorrow," he said.

"Thank you, Unctie," I said.

"Anytime, Princess," he said.

As he left the room, I realized how grateful I was for him. I was so lonely when I came here. I was happy that I met him early enough. I felt like a very small girl in a big city, and this was a very complicated mess. Having him was like having a soft landing, something to remind me that no matter how tough it got, I always had support.

The next morning at the office Diana was literally a robot. She was dishing out orders, not really politely but very authoritatively. Regardless of what was happening between us, I intended to keep this job, so I was very keen on pleasing her. As the others were coming in, I was taking care of them as quickly as possible. When I went for a lunch break, she said, "Good job today, Brenda."

"Thank you very much, ma'am," I said and then headed to the lunch lady.

"Hey, Ms. B," the woman said.

"Hey, Miss Carla," I said. I finally figured out her name after getting the food packs from her every evening for the last two weeks since I started here.

"Today we have some really nice items on the menu. I have taken out some of the best bits, put them in a pack, and kept them in the fridge for you. Let me know when you're ready to go home so that I can hand them to you."

I couldn't be more grateful; she was such a kind woman. "Thank you, Miss Carla," I said. "Someday I'm going to be promoted in this office, and I'm going to buy you all the Doritos you can eat," I said.

"How do you know I love Doritos?" she asked, pleasantly surprised.

I pointed to the corner beside her where all the empty packets lay.

She smiled and said, "You're the most observant person I have ever met, Ms. Brenda, and I'm glad that you work in this office."

I ate my meal in silence, missing Diana the entire time. Why was I missing her? None of this made any sense to me. I didn't know how I felt when it came to her. I knew for a fact that I liked the way she felt on my body, but inside my chest, my heart, I didn't know exactly how I felt. All of this was new territory for me. As a matter of fact, I was still very much surprised at how my body reacted to her. While also trying to navigate why my body was that way, there was no space in me to figure out why my heart was this way.

I didn't want to hurt her, and I also didn't want to hurt myself. Lunch was over, and it was time to return back to her office. When I got to the office, Diana was with another woman. They seemed very cordial with each other, laughing, hitting each other fondly, touching each other, and being all close. I felt really jealous. Did she just say she was falling for me a few days ago? Why was she getting all up close and personal with this woman right in front of me? Was she trying to make me feel bad? Was she trying to make sure I knew that I was expendable?

When I couldn't take it anymore, I stood up and said, "Miss Diana, if you don't need me right now, can I explore the building? I haven't really had time to survey the place since I started working here."

"Oh, that is fine," she said. "As a matter of fact, I'm heading out for lunch with Luna here," she said.

Lunch? She was headed to lunch? I thought lunch was our thing. I needed to get out of the office as soon as possible before my displeasure began to show on my face. I didn't want her to see how jealous I had become. So, I nodded and rushed out of the office. On my way out, I ran into a delivery service with flowers.

"Hi, could you please lead me to Ms. Brenda?" the nice man said.

I froze, wondering who was going to send me flowers. Then I broke into a smile, thinking maybe it was

Diana. Maybe she felt so bad for what I saw earlier. However, I just came out of the office, so maybe she ordered it in the morning. I loved this, but it was so confusing. So, I just told the man, "I'm Brenda. Can I have the flowers, please?" He handed them to me with a note that said, "Congratulations, baby, on your new job."

Now I was worried. I worked with Diana; there was no reason for her to send me flowers with a "Congratulations on your new job" note. Then my phone buzzed, and I got a text message from Luke. It said, "I know you think you can run from me, but the world is so small. I will always find you." I dropped the flowers on the floor and started running. I ran until I got to a coffee shop, and I began to hyperventilate.

I looked around and walked into the coffee shop and sat down. A nice server walked up to me and asked if I needed anything.

With all the strength I could muster, I whispered, "Water, please. Water."

She nodded and came back with a glass of water for me.

"Are you alright, ma'am? Can I help?"

"I don't know. Can you tell me where there's a world that I can run to that my abusive ex will not follow me?" I said.

"Oh, darling, that's a tough one," she said.

"Tell me about it," I said.

After drinking all the water, I called an Uber and started heading home. When I got into the Uber, I realized I had not stopped by the cafeteria to take what Carla had packed for me for my dinner. I was going home to a house where there was no food in my fridge, and I had just used all the extra cash I had left to book this Uber. Tonight was clearly going to be a hungry one.

When I got to the complex, Paxton was standing outside smoking. "Chile, you look like you've gone through a lot today. What's the problem?"

Then, for reasons I could not explain, I began to cry. He pulled me into a hug and said, "Come here, darling, talk to Unctie. We can fix whatever this is."

Without taking a break, as we walked to my room, I began to tell him everything about my day, Diana's behavior with the woman I saw at the office.

He looked at me and said, "Honey, the woman isn't promised to you. She is allowed to see other people.

And yeah, she was a bit of an ass for what she did to you. Doing all of that in front of you was just too much," he consoled me.

It was comforting to see someone understand how I felt, and then I looked away.

"But that was not the only thing that happened today, was it?" he said.

"Oh, I forgot to take the pasta dinner from the lunch lady, so now I have nothing for dinner," I said.

"That's not a problem. I can whip up some pasta for us later for dinner. But again, I suspect that isn't what your problem is," he said.

I looked at him, but before I could say the words, someone knocked at the door.

I stood up and went to open the door, and there he was, staring at me, wearing a very creepy grin, holding yet another bouquet of flowers in his hand—Luke!

I stumbled back into the room, and Paxton stood up and held me steady.

"Who is that?" he asked.

I looked at him and nodded, saying nothing. He knew exactly who that was.

Chapter 6

DIANA

"I know what you're thinking of doing, and it's a terrible idea," Luna had told me. We had seen Brenda take the flowers from the delivery man, and before we could see whatever happened next, Luna ordered me to drive the car.

Our entire dinner was spent with me confiding in her about everything that happened so far: hooking up with Brenda again, having a sleepover, and trying to spend money to take care of her.

"What do you think you're doing?" Luna had grilled me.

"I don't know. I just like how I feel when I'm around her," I rationalized.

"Have you gone insane?" Luna had asked.

"Maybe," I said.

"I need to order a psych eval for you at this point," she said.

"Maybe you should because I feel like I'm going out of my mind," I said.

"Snap out of it!" she yelled at me. When I say yelled, I mean really yelled. In fact, people in the restaurant turned to look at us.

That was Luna. Using embarrassment was not out of bounds in her world. If I needed to be embarrassed to be brought back to my senses, Luna was very well going to embarrass me.

"I don't understand what you're doing, and I certainly don't stand by it. Why are you risking everything that you've worked for over a fling?" she said.

"I have been single for so long. I haven't felt this way about anybody in a very long time."

"You've been hooking up with different women at the bars we have been going to. What is wrong with you?" she asked me.

Then I had to confide in her. "I have been lying. I haven't had anything to do with anybody for the past two years. The first person I've ever been this attracted to was Brenda, which is why it's seeming really hard for me to move away from this, even though I know that I should."

"If you know this is a bad idea, why are you pushing it? There will be other women in the world—women around your age and social status. I mean, we're no longer in the '50s when people were scared to be openly gay. You could definitely find a woman around your age if you actually searched. This obsession with this girl who is way younger and who you're in a position of authority over will not end well for either of you. Stop it now!" she admonished.

I nodded, pretending to accept her advice so that we could focus on our meal. Because she wanted to hear all about my sex life which was now being cut short, lunch eventually spiraled into dinner. That entire time I obsessed over Brenda and the flowers. I couldn't stop thinking about all the possible people who would have been able to send them to her. I thought she said she had been here only recently and had not met anyone else. Was she lying to me?

***

When I got home, it was even worse. I kept thinking about her, and I couldn't even sleep. I tried to text her, but every time I typed the words, I deleted them.

Because no matter how much I wanted to pretend that I could handle this, Luna was right. It was uncharted territory for me, and things could end up really, really badly if I didn't pull away now.

I was not completely invested, so my heart could be saved. But why did it feel like this? Why did it feel like I was drawn to her, even though I knew this relationship could be bad for me? The night was long and tortuous, and I just couldn't wait to get back to work the next day.

I wanted to see her. No, I couldn't talk to her or touch her or do any of the other things we did before. But I could just see her face, even though she never smiled around me anymore. When she came to work this morning, I tried to make a few jokes, but her face remained stoic. She just kept staring into space. When she wasn't working, she seemed too focused on the work to realize that I was there.

"Brenda," I said after a few hours of tortured silence.

She looked up at me and said, "Yes, ma'am."

"Are you alright?"

"Yes, ma'am, I'm fine."

"Could you please stop with the ma'am thing?"

"I'm sorry, Ms. Diana."

"Just call me Diana, for God's sake."

"Alright, Diana."

"Are you okay?"

"Yes," she said.

Then I went silent. She nodded and went back to work. If she was playing a game, it was working. I stood up and left the office, went to my car, and had a smoke break. Though I had not smoked in 10 years, I was so stressed and anxious about everything that I smoked. When I had finished the cigarette, I went back upstairs and said, "We need to talk, Brenda."

She looked at me and said, "Has my work not been satisfactory? Is there something you need?"

"I'm not talking about work, Brenda, and you know it."

"What are you talking about?"

"Our relationship," I said.

She closed her laptop and looked at me, and I finally saw the innocent look she had been covering with this bold demeanor all day.

"What's wrong with you? Why does it seem like you're avoiding me?" I said.

"I'm not avoiding you. I'm inside this office with you, aren't I?" she said.

"Someone can be in the same space with you and still feel distant. I can feel your distance even though I can see you. What is the problem? Did I do something to you besides telling you that I had fallen for you?"

She immediately looked away.

"Brenda, please talk to me. What is the problem? Did I do something?" I asked again.

"No, you didn't do anything, Diana."

"So, what is the problem?" I asked her.

"There's no problem. I'm just dealing with a lot."

"Are you going to tell me what it is you're dealing with?" I asked her.

"No, they are private matters," she said.

"I had hoped that I would be somebody you could talk to when you're dealing with issues," I said.

She nodded and said, "Me too. I can talk to you about stuff, but this one I'd like to deal with myself."

"Can you please give me a hint what is wrong with you?" I said.

"My ex sent me flowers yesterday."

"Your ex? I thought you didn't like him," I said.

"I don't like him, and I don't know how he found me. I'm a little worried that he knows where I work now, since he sent me flowers here."

I felt like somebody had poured cold water on my body after a really hot day in Texas. This was a relief—the person who sent her flowers was not somebody she wanted flowers from. I wish Luna was here to hear this. I soon snapped out of my rejoicing to face the real problem at hand, which was that her abusive ex was back and making plans to re-enter her life against her will.

"Oh wow. Is there something you would like to do about him?" I said.

"Something like what?"

"I mean, we can always get a restraining order against him," I said.

"No, we can't get a restraining order against him because technically he's not harming me. He is just sending me flowers. Most of his damage is emotional, and I can't use that as a means to get a restraining order against him. I'm afraid he will have access to my life as long as he likes.".

I was a little worried. I wanted to help her, but I didn't know how. So, I made a mental note to ask my lawyer friend how we could deal with this issue. Then I said, "Do you want to move to my house for a while? He doesn't know where I live."

She kept quiet and looked away.

"Oh my god, how did he find out where you live?" I said.

"I don't know, but I opened my door yesterday, and he was standing there.".

"Did he do anything to you?" I asked.

"No, he didn't do anything. I had my neighbor with me, and my neighbor chased him away. However, I'm still worried," she said.

"Well, I'm sure this is something that can be fixed. We will find a way. But the offer of moving to my house is still open if you want."

She shook her head and said, "Don't worry about it. My neighbor seems as if he can beat a bunch of people, so I'm going to trust in him to try and protect me from this man."

Then she went back to her work. After a few minutes, she looked up at me and asked, "Who was the woman you were with yesterday?"

"Oh, that's my best friend Luna. She took a small trip out of the country and came back yesterday. We wanted to catch up over lunch," I started saying, and then I froze and looked at her. "Is that why you were all weird yesterday evening and left abruptly?"

She shrugged.

"You were jealous?"

She shrugged again.

"Are you going to keep shrugging or are you going to say something?"

"There is nothing to say," she said.

"It's okay to be jealous, you know. I couldn't focus on lunch yesterday, and I couldn't go to bed like a normal person because I saw you receiving a bouquet of flowers," I said.

She laughed and said, "Are you serious?"

"Yes, I'm serious. I could not stop bitching about it to Luna yesterday."

"I bitched about you and Luna to my neighbor too," she said and started laughing. I started laughing too, until it somehow felt like the ice between us had finally melted.

"I'm not ready for any emotional attachment," she said.

"To be honest, neither am I. But I like how you make me feel, Brenda.".

"I like how you make me feel too," she said.

"So let's leave whatever this is at exploring each other's bodies and enjoying how we make each other feel before we let the complications of emotions and romance cloud it," I said.

"That sounds really good to me."

"Are you sure you don't want to come and stay at my house for now until we figure out what to do about your ex?" I said.

"Don't worry, he's afraid of Unctie."

"Who is Unctie?" I asked.

"He is Paxton, my fairy god Unctie," she said, laughing.

"Gosh! Queer babies are so extra," I said, laughing. I got up from my table and walked around to where she was seated, pulled her into my arms, and kissed her. After we kissed, we spent a few minutes just staying in each other's arms, saying nothing and enjoying the stillness that came with the comfort of being together.

"I don't want to come live in your house, but I can spend a few nights over every now and then," she said.

"Anyway, start tonight. I have missed you terribly."

"Yeah, I was heading there."

"Well, the day isn't over yet. I still have a lot of work to do, so I think this is the part where we move out of each other's arms and get back to work before we do the things that almost got us caught the last time," I said.

We started laughing and pulled away from each other. We got through the rest of the day in a very chipper mood. Anyone who saw both of us working together could tell that something had changed between us. Honestly, we just wanted to finish what we were doing fast enough to go home and devour each other.

Brenda went to the cafeteria, got her lunch, but brought it back into the office to eat with me. I had already ordered Chinese for myself because she insisted on not letting me order for her.

"This Chinese is really nice, you know," I said as I ate my meal.

"I know. It smells nice. So, just order some for me that I will eat at home for dinner," she said.

"You don't want to eat Chinese now, but you want to eat it for dinner?"

"A woman is allowed to choose what she wants to eat. I shall not be forced into eating what you want me to eat for lunch," she said and then broke into a small laugh.

"Fine, you'll have Chinese for dinner, and I will have mac and cheese."

"That's fine. I'll bring the leftover mac and cheese to the office for breakfast tomorrow," she said.

"You have really thought this through, haven't you?"

"You underestimate me."

"Clearly," I said.

Finally, it was closing time, and she rushed out of the office. She walked all the way to the front and waited for me to drive up to meet her so that we could drive home together.

"I have dropped you off at the office before, and that wasn't a problem. Why are you suddenly walking all the way to the front?" I asked her.

"It's simple. If you keep dropping me off every morning and picking me up every evening, or at least almost, these people are going to notice, and start talking. This way, I'm ensuring that I can spend time with you without people talking," she said.

"There is no need for that," I said. "I don't care what people say."

"That's a lie," she said. "You have to care what people say. You have a business to run, and your business is very dependent on reputation. You run a PR agency. Imagine a PR agency having a lot of scandals in-house. Nobody will trust you to clear up their scandal outside," she said wisely.

"Fine," I said. "Walk all the way home if you want."

She nodded.

Four hours later, after many rounds of passion, I went downstairs to the sitting room to get something to eat. I was met with a sight that threw me off balance.

Standing on my patio was my elder brother, holding an envelope. He informed me that he was suing me to take back the company that my father had willed to me before his death.

Chapter 7

BRENDA

It had been six weeks since I started working for Diana, and four weeks since her brother Tommy showed up unexpectedly with a suit to throw Diana out of the company.

I keep remembering the day he showed up like it was yesterday. I was upstairs, and Diana had gone down to get drinks for both of us. But she was down there for so long that I had to go down and find out what was happening. As I went down the stairs, I wanted to call out her name and ask her what was taking her so long. For some reason, I decided to tip toe and sneak up on her instead. Luck had betrayed me as I was naked.

As I tiptoed down the stairs, I heard voices in a heated argument. I knew it was serious and I had to be careful, especially since Diana was not completely clad when she had descended the stairs. I reasoned that if she was going to stand there and argue with somebody in that state, it had to be somebody with whom she was familiar.

As I got closer, I heard her voice clearly. "Our father willed his company to me, Tommy. What are you saying?" she said.

"I was working in the company and overseeing everything in the division for five years before you came out of school and joined us. You had no right to take what was mine," he said.

"I didn't take what was yours. Dad gave us both a task. The task was simple: try to save the PR arm of the company and take it. Those were the rules, and I played by them," she said.

"What stupid rules are you talking about, huh? You think you know better than me because you had a degree in management. I worked for this business for so long, only for my father to take it away from me and hand it to you," he retorted.

"You abandoned the family and the company to go start your own business, and you vowed that you were going to be more successful than all of us. You didn't need the company anymore, wasn't that what you said?" she replied frustratedly.

"Well, I have decided now that I want to merge my company with this one and have everything as I was meant to in the first place."

"I don't understand you. My father split his business into six arms and gave it to his brother, one of our nephews, and the two main companies to our older brothers. Why are you fighting for this one? Why aren't you fighting for the other ones instead? You worked in the entire company. Why are you fighting for this arm, specifically?"

"Because you're a girl, and you shouldn't own anything," he said.

Well, now I was really pissed, and it took so much self-control to keep me on the stairs where I stood. After a heated argument that lasted for an hour, Diana finally said, "I'm exhausted, and I need to go back upstairs and sleep. As you can see, I'm almost naked. But listen to me, Thomas Neville Argon, hell will freeze over in Antarctic-level proportions before I give you my company. You want a fight? Come get it," she said.

Then she turned from him and commanded, "Now get the hell out of my house before I have security throw you out."

He looked at her, smiled, nodded, and said, "You have no idea what you're entering into. My coming to see you was giving you an easy way out of this battle, but if you're saying you want to fight, a fight you will certainly get." Then he turned and walked away.

First of all, I was really turned on by all I had seen. She looked so sexy as she battled on her brother. However, I was also very worried. *Why now? From where had he come, and what did he have that made him think it was possible to fight her?* All of these questions ran through my head. I didn't even realize that I had sat down on the stairs naked.

"What are you doing out here?" she said when she came to the stairs.

"Well, you were taking so long to come back up, and I was worried. But then I came downstairs and realized that you had gotten into an argument. I'm so sorry, I didn't mean to eavesdrop."

"It's okay that you heard it. You already know the story," she said.

"What does he want?"

"He wants the company because he believes girls shouldn't own anything," she said.

"Yeah, I heard that. It was really annoying. Where did he get such sexist and outdated ideas? And where did he get off thinking that was a proper thing to say to you."

"He's about to get the rudest shock of his life because this girl is going to fight for what she owns," she said.

"I'm really proud of you."

"There's a long battle ahead of me, I think," she said.

"Is there anybody you can call in your family to let them know that this is happening?"

"I want to first see what he thinks he has over me and see what strategy he has to take the company before I bring in the cavalry," she said.

"Are you sure you shouldn't just inform them as early as possible to be prepared?"

"Well, that sounds like a good idea, except I don't want to be a bother. So far, I have run the company by myself, and I think this is an adversary that I can take on by myself. In the meantime, let's go figure out what you want to drink and go back upstairs to continue where we left off," she suggested.

"How can you think about sex when you're about to lose your company?"

"When you're looking at me, and you're naked, I can't think of anything else. So maybe when you're all dressed and not looking at me with those eyes, I'll be able to think of the fact that I'm about to lose my company. In the meantime, I have other things on my mind. Let's get our drinks and go upstairs," she said.

I shook my head and said, "You're an interesting woman, Diana Grace Argon."

"I know."

We returned to the room, almost forgetting that the real world existed and that there were issues to worry about.

***

In the two weeks that followed, we realized that this threat was not something to laugh about. It soon became evident that she should have called the family earlier because during the time she waited, Tommy had gone behind her back and bought a significant number of shares in the company. Now, he had just enough shares to tilt the board in his favor and make himself CEO. If she had called her family immediately, her older brothers could have swung into action and bought the majority of shares in the company, ensuring that Tommy couldn't gain leverage.

However, she tried to figure out the issue herself and combed through her entire profile to see if there was something that could be used against her. While she was doing that, she had somehow made the fatal flaw of not analyzing the proportions of shares. Now, she was in a fierce battle to save her company.

Word had begun to spread, and the media was having a field day with this drama. Everyone was trying to figure out who would emerge victorious in this high-stakes game. Tom had moved over to the UK with his business and had been highly successful there. Even the board couldn't question his credentials and whether he could handle the company.

The board consisted of seven voting members. Three of them were in favor of Diana. Three had already been swayed by Tommy, and the last one remained neutral. However, my major concern with him was that he was very conservative. The only reason he still held a position on the board was out of respect for his long-standing friendship with Diana's father and his tenure with the company since its inception. This gave his opinion significant weight. Even more importantly, he was the tiebreaker – the person we needed to convince. The problem was that Diana was a lesbian, and she strongly distrusted him though he did have excellent business sense.

The only people who knew about Diana's sexuality were her friends and maybe a few people in the office. It wasn't common knowledge among the board members as the matter was both private and irrelevant. We felt we had to keep our relationship hidden from the conservative board member if we wanted his vote. With four weeks leading up to the day the board members would cast their votes, Diana was under immense stress.

Inside the office, Luna, Allison, and I sat down with her as she paced from one end to the other.

"Do you think they will keep me if I get the company more deals and make them more money?" Diana asked.

"You have made more money for this company in the last quarter than we have ever made before," Allison said. "I don't think the board is in doubt of your capabilities as a CEO because so far, you've done exceptionally well."

"I know I've done well, but I feel that I need to do even better to retain their trust in me. I can't lose this company to Tommy; it was willed to me! It is my company! I don't know why he wants to take it from me," Diana said, exasperated.

I was frustrated and didn't know how to help. I just sat there, staring at her as she paced from one end of the room to the other, wringing her hands. Diana had always been a very composed woman, always knowing what she wanted to do and how to do it. This was the first time I had seen her so frazzled.

She called her mother on the phone. "Hi, Mom, is there any hope from your end?"

"None at the moment. I've tried to talk to the man, but he's saying that he doesn't want to be swayed by anyone. On the day of the voting, he will go with the one he thinks is more capable of running the company, based on morals and intellect," her mom replied.

As soon as the call ended, Luna spoke up. "I guess we just have to wait and see, don't we?"

"I'm starting to see, and it is just so scary because what are the odds that this will go our way? This can go bad really swiftly, and we would have nothing left," Allison said, expressing her concerns.

Luna turned her attention toward me. "Don't you have anything to say?"

Diana stepped in, saying, "Luna, please don't harass her."

"Believe me, I'm not trying to harass her. I'm just wondering if you have nothing to say regarding all that is going on. She's your assistant, and Allison, you may not know this, but she's also your girlfriend," Luna said.

"Girlfriend?" Diana asked, sounding upset. "We're not that serious yet and thank you for bringing Allison into a matter that didn't concern her. Who else are you betraying me to?"

"What is going on?" Allison asked, puzzled. "Of course, I have the right to know. I work as a manager in this company, and if two people are seeing each other without the notice of HR, it might pose a problem for everyone. Come on, Diana, you're smarter than this. A little slip like this, and if it gets to HR, you'll have to deal with the consequences. You're older than her, you're her boss, everything about this screams unethical and could put you in a position where the board members claim that you're not fit to be the CEO, especially the conservative ones among them."

"Do you think I've not thought of that?" Diana asked.

"I told you that it was going to be a bad idea," Luna said.

"Well, until now…No thank you, Luna… Allison didn't even know about this, and we intended to keep it as quiet as possible. So, tell me, Luna, when and why the heck have you become a turncoat? You know outing people is inappropriate!" Diana declared to her friend.

Luna suddenly felt remorseful, realizing that she shouldn't have said anything. "I'm sorry, Diana. I got carried away. Please forgive me. Even though I'm not in support of this relationship, I see that it makes you so happy, and I should not have said anything, especially in public. But I'm really worried about you losing your company. You've worked so hard for this, and I feel as if this thing you have with her might be a factor. I'm sorry. I should not have voiced my opinion. It was not in my place to talk about it."

"No, Luna, it was not in your place. Opinions are like butts. Everybody has one, and some are better than others. However, none should be shared openly with everyone," Diana said.

Then she looked at me and said, "Get up; we're going home."

I replied, "Go on home. I'll take an Uber and meet you in an hour. I need to figure out a few things here."

When I finally got home, I found her seated on the patio, drinking whiskey and just staring into space morosely. I sat beside her, planted a kiss on her forehead, and then asked, "How rich are you?"

"Why are you asking me that?" she chuckled.

"It's Friday, and I want to take a vacation with you, except I can't afford one, so I'm asking you how rich you are so that I will know if you can afford one and drag you along with me," I said with a playful grin.

Diana started laughing and replied, "Where would you like to go?"

"Hawaii," I said.

"That's great. Let me call my assistant, and tell her I will not be around for the next three days," she said. Then, she picked up her phone, still looking at me, and spoke to "her assistant."

"Hi Brenda, so I'm taking a bit of a vacation, and I will not be around for the next three days. You don't need to do anything, just wait for me until I come back. Thank you."

She ended the call, and we both burst into laughter. In the next two hours, we packed up, headed to the airport, and were on our way to a private island in Hawaii.

Chapter 8

DIANA

We arrived in Hawaii, and it suddenly felt like everything I was worried about had faded into thin air.

"Do you like it here?" she asked me as we lounged on the beach, staring at the ocean smashing against the sand.

"It is peaceful," I said.

"What do you like most about it?"

"That I get to do this," and then I leaned in and kissed her, "in the open."

"Whew! You really do go for the jugular, don't you?"

"You mean like this?" I leaned in, held her throat, looked into her eyes, and then kissed her again, more deeply this time.

"Damn! This feels like a scene out of a smut romance book," she said.

I broke into a small laugh. "Smut? What is that?"

"Wait, you don't know what smut is?"

"I'm sorry: I'm afraid I don't."

"What books do you read?"

"Books that help me," I said.

"Wait, so all of these things are pre-installed?"

"What things?" I asked, surprised.

"Your behavior, the way you look at me, how you hold me, how you touch me?"

"I don't know what you're talking about, but I know that I want to pin you to a wall and have my way with you until you beg for mercy you'll never get," I said.

"Um, come on, we need to get out of here, right now," she said, stood up, and started jogging towards the room.

I ran after her, wondering what was going on with her. As soon as we entered the room, she said, "This is a wall. Here we are. Make good on your threat."

I broke into loud laughter. My first real laughter in months. The whole thing with my brother had put a strain on our relationship, and I had been unavailable. She was working overtime to help me save my company, and we barely had any time for us. I was grateful for this small moment.

"What are you looking at me for, Ms. Argon?"

Ah well, she wanted it, and she was gonna get it. I pushed her to the wall, pinned her with one hand, and knelt before her. I moved her bikini out of the way and planted my mouth on her very moist and salty-from-ocean-water sex and began to suckle softly. She began to whimper and moan softly. I kept at it until her legs began to shake. I steadied her and began to suckle harder. She held onto my head.

"Please—" she screamed.

I looked up and said, "What was that?"

She yelled, "Don't fucking stop!"

"Why, yes ma'am."

I planted my tongue firmly inside her and began to twirl. I was a lesbian in my late 30s. I knew most of the tricks. She screamed louder and shook violently as she came all over my face and then crumbled into a fetal ball on the floor.

I went into the bathroom, washed my face, and came back out to lie beside her on the floor.

"I thought you were joking," she tiredly whispered.

"Oh, girl. Never do that. Never threaten me with a good time. I will always deliver," I teased. I stood up, gave her my hand, and said, "The floor is cold. Come up to the bed. I will order us some food, okay?"

She nodded and got up.

I ordered food. While she was eating, I stepped out to take in some fresh sea air and talk to my mother on the phone.

"Hi, Mama," I said.

"Hi, baby girl. Where are you?" my mother asked.

"I took a small vacation to Hawaii," I said.

"Where do you find the strength to take vacations when your company is on fire, Child?" my mother asked.

"I needed to clear my head. I no longer know what to do. We couldn't get to the shares in time, and Tommy has bought all of them, as you already know. So, some of the stakeholders in the company met up with him to see if they could buy his shares from him at a really high price. However, Tommy says he isn't interested in making a profit; he's solely interested in taking the company from me," I said.

"Your brother Gabriel said that there was an option that you could take advantage of."

"Yes, he mentioned to me that I could merge my company back under the parent company and become a managing director instead," I said.

"Is that an option that you're looking at?" my mom asked me.

"It's a final resort for me. I'm thinking of it."

"I know it feels as if you'll be disappointing your father because he handed over the company to you to make your own. But, he knew that desperate times call for desperate measures, and right now, I think we're all desperate to make sure that Tommy does not get your company," she said.

"I don't understand why Tommy is so angry at me because his own company is thriving. He's literally the top PR agency company in the UK. Nobody can stand in his way. Why does he suddenly want mine?"

"Okay, I think it's high time you knew the true story," my mother said.

"What true story?"

She cleared her throat and said, "Well, here it is. Sometime after having your elder brother Gabriel, I fell into a severe depression, and I was unbearable to be around. The doctors had to take your brothers from me. I participated in in-patient therapy for a very long time. By the time I was well enough to return home, your father had gotten into an affair with his secretary at work. Her name was Louise."

I gasped as she continued.

"I was devastated. Your father begged me not to leave him because that seemed the only option for me. My parents said they were going to support me if I left him. There was nothing holding me back. I had thought I was going to return home to my whole family, but your father's betrayal hurt me terribly. After many more months of therapy and begging from both sides of the family, I decided to give your father another chance, on the condition that he sent Louise far away from the family, and he did."

"Three years later, I got pregnant with you, and while I was pregnant, Louise showed up out of nowhere with a three-year-old boy who was the spitting image of your father. It looked like my world had been turned upside down again. It was bad enough that he cheated on me while I was dealing with one of the worst moments of my life. It was just horrifying that I would have to look in the face of the product of his cheating for the rest of my life. I told your father that he was okay to take care of him, but the boy could not stay in our home. Your father agreed, set up Louise and Tommy somewhere else, paying their bills and making sure they were very comfortable. Their life was almost as comfortable as ours. Then, Louise was diagnosed with cancer and died, so Tommy had to come live with us."

"When he turned 16 years old, your father decided it was time for Tommy to meet his maternal family and learn about his birth. So, he was taken to his mother's sister to stay for a few weeks, which was the holiday he went on when you were younger. While he visited the family, they wasted no time in telling him the entire story, garnishing it with a few lies and exaggerations."

"Most importantly, they told him that I didn't want him to be treated as part of the family. I didn't want him to inherit anything from his father, and that I was not very accepting of him when he was born. They made it seem as if I made his father push his mother away. They told him that if his mother had not died, he would not have moved into the house with us. They told him a lot of things from a very different perspective than ours."

"So, this animosity you see isn't exactly directed at you. It is actually directed at me. However, he doesn't have the power or the resources to fight me, so he's fighting you instead in order to hurt me. I'm really sorry that you have to be the recipient of this madness. You deserve better than this, and I'm going to do everything in my power to ensure that the company stands behind you and fights for you so that this boy does not take what rightfully belongs to you," my mother explained.

"Wow," was all I could manage.

The call wrapped up shortly after, and I felt as if something colossal had been placed on my shoulders. This was way too much information for me to handle. If my mother was right, this battle was not going to end anytime soon because Tommy was not just fighting for a company; he was fighting for legitimacy to the Argon name. That was a battle that I was not sure I could win.

I went back into the room, grabbed a pack of cigarettes, and went outside to smoke. I was beginning to fall back into bad habits. My life was taking a turn for the worst, and I didn't know how to fight it.

"A penny for your thoughts?" Brenda said with a groggy voice. She was just waking up from sleep.

"Yeah, sure…" I said and then I told her the whole story my mother had just told me.

"Oh, that is heavy," she said.

"Yes."

"This also means that he could be playing dirty, if need be. This is much more than we thought it was. He doesn't just want the company; he wants a seat at the Argon table which he can't get because the company was started by both your mom and your dad. If this is true, he doesn't just want your company, Thomas is coming for everything and everyone."

I nodded. She was smart.

"We need to start our research on him immediately. We need to fight back and beat him at his own game, if not we're toast," she said.

Brenda laid on the bed and started thinking. Then she brought out her phone and made a call while I was watching her. As soon as the call was picked up, she put it on loudspeaker.

"Heeeeeey, Unctie," she said.

"Hey, Godchild, I haven't seen you around in a while," he said.

"I'm on vacation with Lady D."

Lady D? I liked that.

"Okayyyyyy, gimme the tea," he said.

She looked at me and winked. "I will, but first, how would you like to make some quick cash?"

"I like the sound of quick money. What do I need to do?"

"Lady D and I have a problem. Someone is trying to take her company, and we need to find some dirt on him. Do you have anybody you think can penetrate his life and get some juicy information for us?" she asked him.

"You have come to the right place, my darling. Of course, I know a lot of people. What's his name? What does he look like? What are his phone numbers and social media contacts?" he inquired.

"I'm going to send that to you in about an hour, and let me know what your price is," she said.

"I'm going to send you an invoice, darling," and then he hung up.

Then she began to type feverishly on her phone, and soon she gathered all the information her Unctie asked for and sent it all to him.

He texted her back with an invoice that said he wanted $2,000. I sent him $5,000. He went to work immediately.

Brenda created a secure email and sent it to him asking him to do the same when sending the info he had found to us, so that neither of us would be indicted if trouble ever happened.

Later we laid on the beach, watching the stars, knowing that our vacation and this peace would soon fade away when we returned to the chaos that was now our life together.

The media was still making a massive spectacle about the take-over of my company, and I was tired of it. Sooner or later, my sexuality was going to come to light, maybe with a video of me at one of the many gay bars that Luna and I had visited. Luna…I was no longer pissed at her, but I needed her to understand that her self-righteous behavior did no one any favors. So, I was going to stay away from her for a little longer.

"What is the best thing that has ever happened to you?" I asked Brenda.

"I don't know. Someday, I will know what it feels like to have the best thing happen to me, but until then, I don't know," she said.

"Are you always this cynical?" I asked.

"No."

I reached out and held her hands.

"What will you do when you have all the money in the world?" I asked again.

"I will take you to dinner at a very fancy place," she said.

"That's a really small goal," I said.

"Well, the smaller the goal, the easier it would be to accomplish," she said.

"I can't fault you on that one."

"You can't fault me on any of my philosophies," she said.

"Why do you say so?"

"Because I'm probably the most realistic person you know," she said.

"For your age, maybe."

"Fair enough," she said.

After a long silence, I said, "I don't want to go back home."

"Me and you both, Brenda," I said.

"But we have to go back home and figure all of this out so that we can take a much longer vacation after it's all over," she said.

"You know we can figure out our relationship better then," I said.

"Maybe we can," she said.

"I really love spending time with you," I admitted.

"Me too," she replied.

The next morning, we got on our flight and returned to New York to face the demons that awaited us. What we didn't realize was that in the short time we took away from the battleground, Goliath had grown bigger. As soon as we got to the office, Brenda received a package. It was from Luke, her ex-boyfriend, and it contained pictures of both of us in Hawaii.

Chapter 9

BRENDA

I paced from one end of Diana's living room to the other, wringing my hands as I went. I was beyond worried. Paxton and Diana were there. She was at one end of the room making calls and trying to solve the issue, while I was worrying.

"Sit down, Chile," he demanded.

"Sitting down won't change anything right now. If Tommy gets his hands on that document, everything Diana has worked for could go down the drain," I said.

"Pacing from one end of the room to the other like an insane person isn't going to do anything right now either. Sit down," Paxton said again.

"Do you know where Luke gave me that document? Do you know that he sent someone to give me that document at the freaking airport? He was waiting for me," I said.

"I wish a lot of bad things for him! All I ever wanted to do was escape him, and right now he's ruining my life and the life of someone I really care about."

I looked over at Diana. She was really frustrated, and this was taking its toll on her. I needed to do something, but I wasn't sure what I could do to fix it.

A few minutes later, Luna and Allison arrived. Luna seemed enraged, and I could see it in her eyes as soon as she came in. Diana immediately ended the call and walked straight to her, saying, "No, no, you will not do that! Don't you look at her that way, harassing her. Don't start with that self-righteous bullshit! I get it, you warned me this was a bad idea, and you think you are trying to protect me. If you don't want to be here to support me, you can leave! You will not hurt her, and you will not make me feel worse!"

I was grateful that she defended me, but part of me wanted to be punished for this. I felt as if my entrance into her life had ruined every single thing that she had ever worked for. I felt as though I should have left the company as soon as I recognized who she was and what we had done, but I stayed. Even when I could have discouraged her from chasing after me, I didn't, and I regretted it.

"I'm not mad at her. I'm mad at the situation," Luna said.

"We all are," Allison added. "Okay, first things first, we need to meet with HR tomorrow and find out what the verdict will be. Oftentimes it means that the one in authority has to take a suspension, but there has to be some other option, considering that we're in delicate times."

"What other option do we have?" I asked.

***

"You will have to quit your job," HR said to me the next day at the meeting.

"Of course not," Diana interjected.

"This is the only way," Allison said.

"Diana, I will do it. It doesn't matter. I will stay at home for as long as you need to fix this mess. I'm not running away," I said.

"There has to be another way," Diana argued.

"There is no other way," HR said and added, "Listen, Diana, I really like you. I don't want to see anybody else running this company. It's yours, and you've been running it efficiently. You've put us at the apex of the business. In fact, some of our employees seem almost untouchable by other companies because they are so skilled and how people view the business that you've created. This company does not deserve to lose its CEO. That is the only reason that I'm willing to look the other way. However, if she remains in this company, it's going to cause a bigger scandal when the news begins to spread."

"Do you not think that it will seem suspicious that my assistant suddenly left the company in the middle of my crisis?" Diana asked.

"Fine," HR said, "let her stay with the company. Brenda, you should move to another department, do a rotation, and have somebody else come into this position, a male this time around."

Then I looked at Diana, and she mouthed the words "I'm sorry."

What was she sorry for? It was Luke, my ex, who decided to ruin everything for her. All of this drama was coming from my end, and she had nothing to be sorry for. She had been absolutely amazing and had not caused me any trouble. I had to find Luke, and I had to do it immediately.

"It would seem to go without saying, but I will say it for the record. You two should not be found near each other unless there is a third-party present– no elevator meetups, hidden meetups, or even home meetups. As a matter of fact, we need both of you to stay completely away from each other until all of this boils over. The vote is in a few weeks, and your records need to stay as spotless as possible until then, Diana," HR emphasized.

"Understood," I said.

"Effective immediately, Brenda Jenkins, you're moved to the data department. Barry Lockhart, one of the new interns, will be taking over your assistant position. Allison, you'll train him. Diana, nothing happens to your managerial position; it remains. We can't have Brenda training Barry. Brenda cannot be around Diana at this moment. Is that clear?" HR directed.

"Yes," Allison replied.

"You both can leave. Diana, stay back; we need to talk," HR said.

As soon as we left the meeting, I went to my office, which was always beside Diana's office, packed every single thing that was mine, and moved straight to the data office. I didn't even want to see my replacement.

When I got there, I told them I needed to go home because I had a stomach ache, and they let me go.

When I got to the door of my house, Paxton was there waiting for me. I had sent him a long voice note, crying on the Uber ride home.

"You should have let me send that boy to hell when he came here the last time," he said. I held him, and I cried even harder.

The next few weeks were the craziest I've ever encountered in my life. I was starting all over. I was in a department that I knew nothing about. I had no business in data. The only other option was being without a job in New York and living from hand-to-mouth again, and I could not afford to do that. I had to put my head down and learn data collection even though I had knowledge or interest in it.

I tried to avoid the floor that Diana was on. Every now and then, I would see her through the glass. She was so focused on saving her company that she wouldn't see me. I felt completely useless. We couldn't text; we couldn't talk on the phone or even be close to each other. My heart ached in unimaginable ways, and for the first time in my life, I contemplated doing something really bad to escape the pain.

One day after work, as I was walking down to the bus station, a nice car stopped in front of me. The door opened. It was Luna.

"Get in," she said.

"Where are you taking me?" I asked.

"I don't like you, but it doesn't mean I want to harm you. You're a young girl, and I don't like you based on principle."

"Why are you being such an ass to me? I have done nothing wrong," I said.

"I know you've done nothing wrong, but it's easier to be mad at a stranger than at my friend," she said.

I shrugged, understanding her perspective to some extent.

"How are you?" she asked.

"Miserable," I replied.

"I'm sorry," she said.

"Where are you taking me?" I asked again.

"I just wanted to have a conversation with you," she said.

"About what?" I asked.

"Did you ever feel as if Diana was taking advantage of you?" she asked.

"Why do you ask me that?" I inquired.

"Because Diana had said that you were straight before you met her," Luna replied.

"Luna, look at me. Do I look the least bit impressionable?" I asked.

"No, you don't," she admitted. "However, when this comes to light, people are going to ask you if she took advantage of you."

"I'm going to tell them *no* every single time because she didn't," I assured her.

After we drove for another thirty minutes, I asked again, "Please, where exactly are you taking me? I'm a little confused. You said you wanted to ask me a few questions, and I feel like you already have. I have answered them all. I would like to go home. I have an early day at work tomorrow."

"I know you have an early day at work tomorrow, and I will drop you off at your apartment complex soon, so be patient," Luna said.

We drove into a pasture leading towards a few bushes. When we got to a small cottage, Luna told me to get out of the car. I began to get really scared about what was about to happen. Just as I got out of the car, I saw Diana run out of the cottage. All my worries immediately disappeared, and I ran into her arms.

I looked up quizzically at Luna. She smiled and said, "You looked really miserable, both of you. I figured I had to bring you both together at some point."

"Thank you so much, Luna," Diana said.

"Am I forgiven now, Diana?" Luna asked.

"It's still under consideration. Maybe if you bring me some food, I will forgive you," Diana said.

"Well, I already got some food, so can I have my forgiveness now?" Luna said as she walked to the back of the car, opened the trunk, and brought out four big bags of groceries, drinking water, and alcohol.

"Be good, both of you. I'll be back to pick you up in two days," Luna said before driving away.

As soon as Luna left, Diana lifted my face up to hers and kissed me. I had never felt more complete in my life. It felt like every single thing that I had ever missed was right here in my arms.

"I really hate the data department," I said to her.

"I really hate Barry," she said to me, laughing.

Then she kissed me again.

"What's going on? I hear nothing. Nobody tells me anything," I said.

"We're in the middle of closing a very important deal, so the board decided to move the vote to two months from now. That gives us time to figure all of this out," she explained.

"I have missed you so much," I said.

"I have missed you too," she said. "I needed to see you. I was so miserable, and I didn't even have to say anything to Luna. She simply brought me here and told me to rest. She knew that I had a tough day. I thought she was going out to get us some drinks and snacks. I didn't know that you were part of the drinks and snacks that she was bringing."

I laughed and said, "I'm grateful she brought me."

"Come on, let's go inside," Diana said. "There's a lot we need to catch up on," and she winked.

A few minutes later, clothes were strewn all over the floor while we were entangled in a heated romance on the bed. Diana made me lie on my side. Then she pushed my legs apart and moved her legs between mine. She kept adjusting till both our sexes were touching each other. She reached into her bag and brought out a small lube which she had always carried around since Hawaii.

She spritzed some on me and then on her. It felt cold and pleasurable at the same time. Then she told me to hold on, which, of course, I was already doing. She held onto me and began to move in an up and down motion. As she did, I felt a warm sensation in my lower abdomen, and the pleasure began.

I had read about this in my smut romance books, but nothing, absolutely nothing prepared me for what was about to happen to me. I could feel the world around me disappear as she moved. Then I grabbed onto her and increased my rhythm to match hers. As we went on, I began to moan, as did she. Finally, we reached a satisfying climax together and stayed in each other's arms.

As night fell, we stepped out of the cottage and sat down by the small lake beside it.

"I wish we had met at a later time," I said.

"What later time?" she asked.

"I don't know, maybe after I had found a job in New York, and it wasn't in your office," I replied.

"Do you believe in fate?" she asked.

"No, it's not realistic. But why do you ask?" I inquired.

"I think we met when we were meant to meet. Any slight alteration in our universe would have pushed us apart," she said.

"Does that mean that we would have never been together?" I asked.

"Possibly. It does not mean that we would have been unhappy, just that we would have found someone else," she explained.

"That's an interesting thought process. You don't believe that people are meant for each other?" I questioned.

"No, I believe that you find someone and make them your one. I don't think anybody exists to be anybody's one," she replied.

"Do you think that I'm your one?" I asked her.

"I don't know right now, but I know that time will tell. I also know that people work hard at a relationship to become each other's one," she said.

"Is that what this is, a relationship?" I asked her.

"What do you want it to be, Brenda?" she asked me.

I looked up at the millions of stars above us. They were so beautiful. I reached out and held her hand, saying, "I never want to be apart from you, Diana." In that moment, in her arms, I realized for the first time what it truly meant to love a woman.

"Me neither, Brenda." she said.

"So, what do we do?" I asked. That was a silly question because I knew what needed to be done. While she slept, I got out my phone, and I texted Luke, *"What do you want?"*

Chapter 10

DIANA

Brenda and I had returned to our lives at work. Of course, we were still staying away from each other because we didn't want to fuel rumors, and we were being careful. Nonetheless, I had been keeping an eye on Brenda, and something was definitely wrong with her. She was taking calls constantly in the lobby. She left as soon as the work day and even forgot to take her dinner from the lunch lady. She was acting really shifty.

Something was definitely going on with her, and it was killing me that I could not ask. I tried to get Luna and Allison to find out what was going on with her, but they were very adamant about not helping me out by sending messages to her. When it seemed as if I was becoming a nuisance, they collectively decided that it was time for me to go home to my family.

Earlier in the week my mother had called, asking me to come home because we were having a family meeting with Tommy and his aunty, to see if this problem could be resolved amicably to avoid the dirty fight that was looming over us.

I wanted to tell Brenda, but since her shifty behavior began, I decided that I was going to figure out why that existed first. It seemed, though, that I had no time to do that now. My company needed saving.

After watching her for a while, I packed up my things and headed home to my family home in Tennessee. My parents had retired there when the company had been split into four arms for my brothers and me. Now it had only three arms because Tommy refused to handle the talent agency and was so interested in taking my company that Gabriel had to collapse it under his media production arm.

As soon as I arrived home, I felt a sense of peace wash over me. I immediately wished Brenda was here and brought out my phone to text her but held back. We had been advised by HR to no longer text each other, for if investigations were launched into our phones to prove an inappropriate relationship had taken place, I would be a sitting duck. I missed Brenda so much, and I was worried about her. The sooner I fixed this company issue, the sooner we could get back to being lovers.

I entered the house and fell into my mother's open waiting arms. "Mama," I said.

"Oh, baby. You have been through so much. Come on now, Carla has made us dinner. There are freshly pressed grapes in a jar in your room.

Go on up and freshen up, take some nap and join us for dinner, will you?"

I nodded and went up to my room. As soon as I got into the room in which I had grown up, a wave of nostalgia hit me. My bed was just the way I left it years ago. My father had ensured that I had a king-sized bed in my bedroom because he wanted me to always come back to the familiarity of home. I insisted on having a small Barbie bed, but my father refused. He said to me, "If I get you the small bed now, when you grow up, you'll need a bigger bed. Then changes will need to be made. I want you to always come back to a place that feels like home, where nothing has changed."

Looking back, I appreciated that he did this because if there was anything I really needed right now, it was the familiarity of falling back on the bed that I had slept on since I was seven years old. It had the same colorful bed sheets that I had as a child. My mother had laundered them and spread them back on the bed for me. I immediately lay down on the bed and pulled my blanket over myself. I knew my mom would freak out if she saw me wearing my outside clothes in the bed, but I was sure she would understand.

After a few minutes of basking in that comfort, I walked into the bathroom and had a nice, cool shower. Again, I wished Brenda was here because I would have loved to show her every single thing in this room. It felt like walking into a time capsule. After a long shower, I finally climbed into bed and texted Luna and Allison. I told them that I had arrived and asked them to look out for Brenda for me, and then I shut my eyes and went to sleep.

I woke up a few hours later, refreshed, feeling peachy, and most importantly, famished. I remembered that my mother had kept a jar of freshly pressed berries for me and drank some of it. Then I changed into something more appropriate and went downstairs for dinner. When I got down, I met my brothers Gabriel and Dean. I ran to hug them immediately.

"Hey, Bunny, you look like you had quite a month," Gabriel said.

I nodded, feeling like a child.

"Come here," Dean said, pulling me into a tighter hug. "Don't worry; you're home now. All of this will be fixed," Gabriel reassured me.

"Mom told me that Tommy was not our real brother."

"What do you mean? He's our real brother," Dean said.

"You know what I mean," I retorted.

"Yes, we know what you mean," Gabriel said. "However, when Tommy came back from the holiday with his auntie, he began to act really weird. So, we decided that there was no need for us to tell you about the problems with him. We didn't want to ruin your memories of him, because we knew how that felt as ours were already ruined."

Tommy had come back from that vacation being a very different person. He was colder towards everyone in the house, snapped often, spent more time in his room, and yelled at my mother more often. Gabriel tried to keep him in check a few times, but it always spiraled into a fight.

My father tried his best to keep his boys away from each other. Whenever I asked my mother why Tommy was behaving that way, she simply said that he was a boy.

Sometimes boys behaved strangely. I believed her. It didn't help that I was a teenager who was coming to terms with my sexuality, realizing that I didn't really like boys. So, whatever my mom told me about Tommy just being a boy made sense to me. In my opinion, boys were indeed stupid.

I paid no attention to what was going on with him then. In a way, I felt responsible, which made me feel guilty. Maybe if I had been nicer to him, he would have left me alone.

My father had asked him to take over the talent agency while I was still in university. He said he didn't want it because it was still in the early stages and there was no funding for it at the time. Since there was no funding, my father was not ready to pour money into it because he didn't think it was going to be a profitable venture. Gabriel told my father that he was going to see how to make it profitable and asked my father what he was going to do with the company if it became profitable. My father agreed that Gabriel could take over the company, building it from scratch.

On the other hand, the PR arm of the business had a lot of funding, and Tommy said he wanted that one. I told him that I was in school studying communications with a major in PR to take over that arm of the business. However, if Tommy wanted it, then he could battle me out for it with ideas on how to push the business forward. Tommy had no knowledge of how to run the business, and I did. So, while I was working on a business plan, Tommy was trying to lobby my father into giving him the inheritance because he was the boy, and I was the girl. Tommy finally gave up trying to convince him and decided to go to school and learn communications so that he could take over the company. In the meantime, I presented my business plan to my father, and he thought it was a good idea. Dad let me run that branch of the company.

However, before Tommy could graduate, my father died. Naturally, because the company was already in my name, it was bequeathed to me. The official separation of the arms of the business began, with all of us taking our piece to run the way we wanted. After graduation, Tommy left the country to start a PR agency in the UK, which was successful. We thought that was the end of his antagonistic behavior until he came back to fight me for my PR company.

I had always been confused by his isolation from the rest of the family until my mother told me the entire truth. Then everything suddenly made sense, but it also made me sad. For the longest time, he had felt as if he was an outsider in his own family. He was punishing all of us for his suffering.

"Come on, let's go eat," my mother said, and we all sat down around the table.

"Who's going to say grace?" Mom asked. Dean cleared his throat and held Gabriel's hands, who held my hand, and then I held Mom's.

Then he said, "Father, we thank you for this food. We thank you for bringing the family together today. Please help us to solve the problems that finally brought us together so that the next time we gather together, it's not because we have a problem to solve. Amen."

We all said amen, with Mom saying the loudest amen, and we all started laughing.

As we ate, Mom looked at me and said, "So, tell me, Diana, who are you seeing?"

"That was so out of the blue, Mom," I said.

"Well, who is she?" she probed.

I froze, and I looked at my brothers. They knew about my sexuality, but I didn't think they were going to tell my mother.

My mother looked at them and said, "You both knew, and nobody told me?"

I looked at my mother and said, "Wait, how did you know?"

"Child, I gave birth to you, and I lived in this house with you for twenty years before you got your own apartment and moved to New York. I know when my own child is gay. So, tell me, who is the pretty woman you're seeing?"

I hesitated for a bit, and then I began to talk. I described Brenda, talking about her eyes, her hair, and how she made me feel. However, I failed to mention that she was an intern in my office and that she was way younger than me. Moreover, I didn't bring up the fact that somebody was blackmailing us with her pictures. That was too big a problem to bring to the family table, considering how much we already had to deal with.

We spent the next few minutes laughing about our relationships, our childhood, and many memories. Even though Tommy wasn't here, it still felt like home. Then he showed up to our dinner with his auntie, and they started clapping dramatically.

"I see the family has gathered without me," he said.

Mother looked at him and replied, "Tommy, behave respectfully; you're late."

He retorted, "Well, I had some business to attend to. I wasn't going to come here for niceties anyway, so there was no need to arrive early. Anyway, thanks for the offer."

He looked at his auntie and said, "Please sit down." Then, we all sat down at the dinner table. I remained silent, just staring at my plate.

Then he said, "I didn't come here to explain anything to anyone. I just came here to say one thing: I'm not backing down, no matter what happens."

"Tommy, what is wrong with you?" Gabriel asked him.

"What is wrong with me? Do you think that the family cutting me out isn't enough to get me angry?" he asked, outraged.

"No one cut you out; you cut yourself out! Dad thought to give you a fair deal more than once. You didn't want to handle the talent agency of the company that you were offered. You were not supposed to battle out the ownership of this company. It was originally our sister's company, as a matter of fact; but because you wanted it, Dad asked you to make an effort. You refused to do even that. You wanted something handed to you and did not want to work for it. How were you supposed to run a business you had no knowledge of?" Gabriel bellowed.

"Now, I have knowledge of the business, and I'm back to take it. Everybody keeps crying about it. She should just move out of the way and let me handle the company like I wanted to. I could then merge it with my company in the UK, and we can run the firm from both ends. She can be the managing director when I'm not in the US, but she shouldn't have a name on that company as if it's hers, because it's rightfully mine," Tommy asserted.

"It's not rightfully yours, you ingrate," I finally spoke up.

"Finally! She speaks," he said. "I thought you were going to let your brothers do all the talking for you, just like you let Daddy do the talking for you back then."

"I see this dirty game you're playing. I'm not going to play it with you. I'm better than you," I said.

"You're not better than him," his auntie, who had been silent the entire time, eventually said.

Mama was not going to have it. She looked at her and said, "You should know that Tommy is the only one of you that can be considered family at this table. To me, you're a stranger and an intruder in my home. You will not talk to my daughter with disrespect. You will keep quiet until you're spoken to, and if you can't handle these rules, please leave my home."

She stood up, and Tommy stood with her as they headed for the door. Just before they left, Tommy turned to face the table where we were seated and said, "Just so you know, I'm not just coming for her PR company. I'm coming for every single one of you, so sit tight. I'll get what was due to me and what was due to my mother." Then he turned and walked away.

Dinner was ruined.

***

The next day, I packed up my stuff against my mother's wishes and headed back home. My brothers did the same thing. If Tommy was coming for all of our family's business, then we all needed to fight.

I said goodbye to my family and caught the next flight to New York. When I arrived in New York, the first person I wanted to see was Brenda, but I couldn't see her the way I wanted to. So, I wore a hooded jacket, got into a town car, and headed to her apartment complex.

I stood in front of her apartment complex for an hour, waiting for her to come out, but she never did. Just as I got back into the town car, I saw her get out of a cab with a young man. They walked right into the complex together, his hand on her lower back.

Chapter 11

BRENDA

"I didn't agree to get back together with you. I agreed to have dinner with you and talk, Luke!" I yelled.

"Why do you think I wanted to have dinner? For fun?"

"I don't care why you wanted to have dinner. When I texted you asking you what you wanted, you said one dinner. That one dinner has now turned into four, and you insisted on coming back to my house with me. I need you to let me be, please." I begged.

"I can't let you go," he yelled back.

"Why? I have moved on; I have a new life here!"

"With the woman you're seeing?"

I froze and shut up. Diana being mentioned was enough reason to make me keep quiet. I didn't know how much he knew, and I was not going to give him any ideas. I simply looked away.

"Cat caught your tongue?" he asked. I refused to answer and walked to another end of the lobby and crouched on the floor. I was not going to let him see what I was hiding.

"Come to think of it, you freeze every single time I mention your relationship with the woman. Is there something you're hiding from me? Come on Brenny Boo, talk to me." I refused to look at him.

He walked closer to me and said, "I will come by the office to take you for lunch tomorrow, and you best be ready to come with me, no excuses." And then he blew a kiss at me. As he walked out of the room, Paxton was at the door. Paxton would have hurt him, but he knew the power he had over me and Diana, so he restrained himself and settled for a death glare instead.

I ran into Paxton's arms as soon as Luke left the room and began to cry, "Oh, my darling. You're really going through it, aren't you?" he asked. I held him tighter and cried even harder. "I could follow him and steal his phone and those photos, you know."

"He would just print out more. We don't know all the places that he has those photos stored."

"Well, that is a fair point, Chile. I'm so sorry you're going through this, boo."

The next day at work I could barely concentrate. I think my supervisor must have reported me to HR and asked for a switch in interns because I was basically useless, so HR called me to her office. I was already scared of that woman; she seemed very cold-hearted.

"Umm, good afternoon," I said as soon as I entered her office.

"Sit down," she said, without looking at me. I did.

"Do you realize that an appraisal is done for interns at the end of their first six months here to determine if we should keep them or let them go?"

"No, ma'am," I said.

"Do you also realize that I can't take any review from Ms. Argon because of your alleged relationship with her?" I nodded. "Is there a reason you're intentionally trying to ruin your career at Uptown Agency and possibly everywhere else?"

"I'm sorry," I whispered.

"Speak up, child."

"I'm sorry," I said louder.

"I don't want an apology; I want to understand what you're doing and why."

I said nothing. She continued. "As far as I know, this was not a real relationship, the both of you were simply having sexual relations. It should be easy for you to get out of it, shouldn't it? Why are you acting like a lovesick kitten?" I said nothing still, fighting tears.

"Consider this a warning, Ms. Jenkins. If I get one more complaint from the data department about your rotation there, you'll be let go as you've become a waste of company resources. Is that understood?" she asked.

I nodded.

"You can get on with your day," she said.

I stood up and walked out of her office and staggered into the storeroom, crumbled to my knees and cried my heart out. I stayed in this position, crying, and didn't know when Allison entered.

"Oh dear," she said as soon as she saw me.

I struggled up to my feet and tried to run off.

"There is no need to do that, love. It is just me," she said, and pulled me into a hug. "This is really hard on the both of you, isn't it?"

I couldn't mouth the words in my heart. I wanted to ask her how Diana was, and ask her to tell Diana that I missed her terribly. But, I couldn't. So, I just held onto her and cried instead. When I finally had my fill of tears, I pulled away from her and headed back to my office.

I walked up to my supervisor later and said, "I'm sorry I have been dead weight around here, I will pick up.

"To be honest, it does nothing for me. I just thought you would be more than willing to earn your place here. I'm sure you were not rotated here because you were incompetent. Pick up the slack, and get to work," he said and walked away. I nodded and went to meet a fellow intern, Rodney.

"Hi, Rodney," I said.

"Hey, Morose," he replied.

"What is that?"

"My nickname for you," he said.

"Why?"

"You're always staring morosely," he said.

"Oh, well. Could you please explain some of the tasks we do here to me? I'm struggling somewhat."

"I can see. How about we have lunch together, and then we can work on it? I can't tutor you while we're working, I can only show you the basics, but I can teach you how things work during lunch," he said.

"Start tomorrow?"

"What happened to not putting off for tomorrow what you can at least start today?" he asked.

"I have an engagement for lunch already today."

"Okay, cool. Tomorrow, then."

I took a deep breath and went to my seat, trying to make sense of everything that was happening to me.

A few minutes later, my phone buzzed. It was Luke. He was outside waiting for me. I grabbed my jacket and went outside. This was my life now—missing the woman I loved and not being able to talk to her despite being an elevator's distance away from her. Getting queries at work. Begging a fellow intern to be my teacher and having lunch with my ex-turned-blackmailer. This was my life now, a roller coaster of shitty events.

I got outside and met Luke, who was smiling at me and holding a bouquet of flowers. I took the flowers from him and got into the car. I looked up and saw Diana from the glass, having a conversation with Allison. I sighed and looked at Luke.

"Why won't you leave me be?"

"Because you're deceiving yourself into thinking that you can be away from me," he said.

"Luke, you kept cheating on me. You kept breaking my heart. You gave away my mom's fabric to a random girl."

"Well, I didn't know that she had it on," he said.

"Luke, please let me be happy."

"You can be happy with me."

"I can't."

The car stopped. "We have gotten here. Fix your face, and calm down. I don't want people to think I was punishing you."

"But you are."

"Calm down, Brenny," he said.

I calmed down, and we walked into a restaurant together. We ate in silence, mostly because I zoned out so that the torture called "lunch" was going to finish soon without any participation from me. Luke, on the other hand, kept chattering about what our life was going to be like together. After an hour of what was the most torturous lunch in my entire life, it was finally over with my meal untouched.

"I do have to get back to work."

"You do know that when we finally get married, you'll have to come back home with me," he said.

"My home and my life are in New York now."

"No, dammit! Your home is with me!" he snapped.

I stopped talking and just looked outside the window.

"You look really sad," he said.

"Is this a joke?"

"What do you mean by that?" he asked.

"You do things to make me sad, and then you look at my face and tell me I'm sad. Are you trying to rile me up or something?"

"I'm not trying to rile you up. I want to take you back home with me, make you my wife, and have beautiful children with you. I don't want to do it by force," he said.

"If you don't want to do it by force, why are you blackmailing me and Diana?"

"Because I see that you're going down the wrong path, and I want to bring you back to the right one," he said.

"So, the right path is with you, and the wrong path is with the person that I actually like. that does not make sense."

"You're in your twenties. I can see that you're exploring. You're not gay. You're a straight woman, and you're meant for me," he said.

"If I were seeing a man, would you be going around taking pictures of us? As a matter of fact, how did you even know we were in Hawaii?"

"Well, I followed both of you to the airport," he said.

"What does that even mean?"

"I followed you from your office in your Uber. I thought you were going home. I wanted to meet you at home and talk to you. But then I saw you stop at this strange place. It was a really nice building, and I was wondering what you were doing there. So, I stayed outside and waited. Then all of a sudden, you came out with a woman. You seemed really cozy with each other. Initially, I thought she was a friend, but then you got to the airport and booked a flight. I did the exact same thing and remained at the back while both of you went all the way to first class. When you arrived at the island in Hawaii, I followed both of you until I started seeing you kiss on the island. That was when I knew that you had been drawn to the wrong path. It is okay to explore, as I said. But, that has to end now. This is real life, and in real life, you're mine," he declared.

"Yours?" I asked and then broke into a witch-like cackle. "Tell me, the pictures that you took of us, how do you intend to use them ?"

"I'm going to send them to your parents to tell them that this is what has become of you unless you come back with me," he replied.

"So, the reason you took the pictures was so that you could show them to my parents? Are you serious?"

"What else should I be doing? Looking at them makes my life even more miserable," he replied.

It took everything in me to not break into laughter at that moment. So that was why he wanted the pictures—to show them to my parents. It wasn't because he wanted to ruin Diana's life. Gosh, I needed to tell her this, but I was still banned from texting her. I needed to celebrate with someone, though.

"Please take me back to my office. I need to get back to work," I said, laughing.

"Why are you laughing? What is suddenly funny?" he questioned.

"You, you're funny. I'm not going back with you, and I'm not getting back into a relationship with you. Whatever you intend to do with those pictures, be my guest."

"I'm going to show them to your mother and father," he said.

"What do you think will happen? Do you think they will cut me off?   If you're not going to take me out of here, I'm going to leave by myself. Either way, I'm getting out of here today, on my own terms. So, shall we?"

He stood up and said, "I would really like you to consider this better."

"I don't know what you want me to consider. You want me to get back together with you. You didn't even try talking it out. You started by threatening me, showing up at my house, following me all the way to Hawaii while I was on vacation, taking pictures of me with somebody else, and going as far as trying to blackmail me. If you're trying to get me to forgive you, you've done a pretty terrible job of it."

"What can I do to fix it, please?" he inquired desperately.

"There is nothing you can do to fix this except take me back to my office and leave me alone. Keeping me here is just going to make matters worse."

"Can we at least be friends?" he said.

"First things first, delete those pictures from your phone. I also need those hard copies that you have. Bring them to my house, and then we can have a conversation. Until then, do whatever you want with them. Ostracize me from my family because you know how religious they are. Tell everyone back at home that I'm going around New York with an older woman. I don't care."

"Fine, I will delete them," he said, took out his phone, and deleted the pictures.

I didn't trust him, but knowing that he was not an immediate threat was important to me. I definitely needed to tell Diana this. I hated that I was banned from talking to her, but there were worse things than this.

When we eventually got to the office, he looked at me and said "I really do love you, and I want us to grow a family together. I know that I have messed up in the past, and I also know that I went about this the wrong way. There was no reason to blackmail you and the woman that you were seeing. I really do believe that your place is with me, and I know that in time you will realize that. I'm going to be here waiting when you do."

I got out of the car with a big smile on my face and walked towards my office. I heard him call my name, and I turned to look at him. He handed me the flowers and said, "Take these at least. I know that you used to love peonies."

He was right. I did love peonies, and my new desk at the drab data office required some picking up. So, I took the flowers, bid him goodbye, and headed to my office. I couldn't wait to get home and celebrate with Paxton.

"I can't believe we were all frazzled and went into lockdown mode on our relationship because of a mere coincidence," I said to Paxton as we walked into the gay bar. He had offered to take me to the bar to celebrate, seeing as I could not reach out to Diana to tell her.

There was one less demon to worry about, so I was fine with celebrating.

We had just entered the club when I saw Diana dancing with a woman around her age. It wasn't Luna. This woman was unknown to me. It reminded me of the first time Diana and I ever danced together. Paxton saw her too, held me, pulled me out of the bar, and took me home.

Chapter 12

DIANA

"I'm sorry. I just can't," I said to the beautiful date that Luna had scored for me earlier. She wanted me to stop "mourning" my relationship with Brenda after seeing all that had happened with her and the strange man with whom I had seen her going on dates.

I had refused countless times, but when I saw Brenda go out for lunch with him and come back smiling with flowers, I knew that I had to move on. It was a bad move to ever go out with someone that young in the first place, especially because she wasn't even a lesbian.

I had my company to focus on, and Tommy was still making moves behind me. He had graduated to talking to my clients to get them to lose confidence in me. If our clients began to back out, it would force the hand of the board. They would have no other option but to vote. When they did that, it would be at a time when they were losing confidence in me. My brother was really playing his hand. I had no time to be worried about someone who moved on so fast from me.

She never did answer when I asked her about a relationship, so I guess that was it. When Luna pressed on me again to go out, I saw no reason to refuse her, so I went. Here I was with this woman, and all I could do was think of Brenda. Her name was Clarisse, and I had called her Brenda four times already tonight.

"You can't what?"

"I can't do this. I'm not ready," I said, tearing up.

"So why are you out here?"

"My friends think I should come out more."

"What about this Brenda person you seem to be missing her so much?"

"Well, she isn't missing me," I said.

"I'm sorry you're going through this, but I don't want to be your in-the-meantime person."

"I understand," I said. "I'm sorry for wasting your time. I'm going to head to my car."

"Wait, friends?"

"Friends," I replied, and then I got in my car and drove off.

***

The next morning in the office, Luna burst into my office with so many questions. "How did it go? What happened? Did you like her? Did you guys hook up? Did you dance? Talk to me! What's the story?"

Initially, I ignored her and focused on what I was doing, but she kept pestering me. Finally, I looked at her and said, "I'm not over Brenda, and I would really appreciate it if you stopped trying to hook me up with other women. I'm trying to move on. I'm trying to save my company, and I don't want to go on dates. So, please stop!"

She looked at me for a while and then sat down, exasperated. Then she said, "I don't know what to do with you anymore. You're clearly very sad that your little girlfriend has somehow moved on with her life, and instead of you moving on with yours, you sit here in the office sulking all day."

"You know, if you really want to help me get out of my bad mood, you can try to help me fix my company. That's something you can do for me, not trying to hook me up when I'm clearly not over Brenda. You can tell that I'm not over her. It isn't fair to me, to Brenda, or to the next person."

"You can't keep getting mad at me because I'm trying to help," she said.

"I'm not mad at you because you're trying to help. I'm mad at you because you won't leave me alone. The only thing I need help with is saving my company; I don't need help with my love life".

"What can save your company now?" she asked.

"Tommy is going around and trying to get my clients to pull away from the company. If that happens, then I'm toast. All the board members need to vote against me is a drop in revenue. If dropping revenue or confidence triggers a vote, then that's the end. They will vote me out on grounds of incompetence, which is what he is pushing for. He just needs one more person from my side to tilt. At this point, he doesn't even need the Republicans anymore,"

"So, what are you going to do?" she asked.

"I really don't know. I'm racking my brain, trying to figure it out. The least you can do is not try to distract me, so I'm not completely embarrassed. Can you do that, please?"

"I'm so sorry, Diana," she said. "Regardless of how pure my intentions were, the number one thing to do would be to ask what I need to do. So, now I'm asking you, how can I help?"

"To be honest, I don't really know right now".

"Well, I'm going to order Chinese and make sure you eat while you figure this out," she said.

I almost accepted the gesture. Then I remembered that the last time I had Chinese, I had it with Brenda. It was a pretty cute moment for both of us. I didn't want to be stuck in that memory, so I told her, "Not Chinese, just order anything random, please."

"But, you love Chinese," she said.

"Yes, I love Chinese. I'm just not in the mood to have it today. Can I have something else, maybe Indian curry and bread?"

"Okay, whatever Diana wants, Diana gets," she said, and then she got on her phone and began to make the order.

"I have a meeting," I whispered to her, and then I left the office and headed for the boardroom.

Regardless of what's going on, the company still had to run smoothly as if we were not on fire. That meant meeting for the bi-weekly reports that I usually asked the staff to give me, mainly the heads of departments. It was an important meeting.

On my way to the meeting, I passed by the lunch area and saw Brenda with some guy. They were laughing and talking about something. I had to restrain myself from going in there, asking her what was going on and who the hell this new guy was because he clearly wasn't the same person with whom I had been seeing her.

After watching them for a while, I left and headed for my meeting. Throughout the meeting, I wasn't paying attention. My mind was filled with a lot of questions that I could not ask.

When I got back to the office, I was met by Luna with food and a big smile.

"What are you smiling about?"

"Guess," she said.

"I'm not in the mood for any of your guessing games today. Are you going to tell me what you're smiling about or not?"

"You're so salty and no fun these days," she said.

"Try losing your company and your girlfriend in a very short time, and then come back and talk to me about being salty."

"Fine, fine. You're having such a terrible year, but I may have just helped you solve a small problem. In the grand scheme of things, it's really small, but I'm sure it can help," she said.

"What is it?"

"Well, I put some resources around and got a few top clients from Beverly Hills to sign up with your agency for representation," she said.

"Are you serious right now?"

"I'm not joking. The more deals you get, the more confidence your board members have in you. The more confident they are in you, the better. So have your guys finish up these deals, make some more revenue for the board and the shareholders, including your brother, sadly," she said.

***

"If it is possible, can we hide the original identity of these clients?"

"Yes, it is possible to leave them anonymous while we work behind the scenes, but we will still have their important files," the head of acquisition answered, surprised at the suggestion.

"That is fine, but keep their identities and contact info on a need-to-know basis. The only people who need to know who they are you and the members of your team who are handling their case files. Most importantly, ensure that those people who are handling the files sign a non-disclosure agreement."

"Is there a reason for this?" he asked. "We usually are very open with our clients."

I speculated for a long time in my head if I should tell him what the true situation was. I didn't know who Tommy was working with behind the scenes in my company, and there was nobody I could trust right now. So, I simply said, "Well, this is just something I'm trying out. Some information should not easily get out to the outside world, and we need to monitor how information moves around the company so that we close any possible leaks that breach client confidentiality."

"That makes so much sense," he nodded. "I will keep this very private and limit the number of team members who are in charge of the case files. If there is any leak, I'll come to you with it immediately," he said.

"Thank you very much for your understanding." When I left him, I went back to my office to meet Luna.

"Are you ready to go home?" she asked.

"Yes, I am. Let's go."

On our way out of the office, we saw Brenda walking all the way to the bus station again, but this time she wasn't walking alone. She was walking with the guy I had seen in the office.

I sighed heavily.

"I know you want to be mad at yourself and mad at her, but there really is no one to be mad at in this situation," Luna said.

"Stop with the fake sympathy. I know that you're happy about this."

"I'm not happy about anything that hurts you," she said.

"Well, you can be happy about this one because you did warn me."

"Think of it this way; she's probably trying to cope too because she can't talk to or reach out to you. She feels useless. She has nothing to offer, and I know that she cares about you. I don't know what is going on between her and this boy with whom you've been seeing her, but I know that she's not intentionally trying to hurt you. If both of you could stop, you would see that. I believe that the inability to have conversations because you're trying to protect your brand and her is causing a strain on both of your emotional states. Try not to let it bother you so much. Let's focus on trying to fix your company, and then you can go and have a conversation with her about all of this. I know that you're dying to know," she said.

"Yes, I'm dying to know. Do you think we can we pick her up?"

"Do you think that is a good idea?" Luna said.

"I don't know."

"Well, let me be the first to tell you that isn't a good idea. She's not walking alone; she's walking with another intern. If you stop and suddenly try to pick up one of them, what would you explain to the other person?" she quizzed.

She was right. That was the thing I hated the most at this point about Luna, the fact that she was always right. Maybe she was right about Brenda too. Maybe I was overreacting. Maybe all of this could be resolved with a conversation.

***

I drove to a supermarket.

"What are we doing here?" Luna asked me.

"We're trying to figure out a way for me to talk to Brenda without getting in trouble."

"How do we do that in a supermarket?" she asked me.

"We're going to buy a burner phone."

"Oh wow, that is genius! Why didn't any of us think of that sooner?" she said.

"I don't know, but it just crossed my mind now. So, I'm going to go buy two burner phones. I'm going to call her on one and then have her come and pick the second one."

"Where will she come and pick it from?" Luna asked.

"She will come and pick it from wherever she says she can meet you up."

We went into the supermarket, and I bought two burner phones. When we got home, I showered and changed. I went through the entire conversation that I wanted to have in my head, and then I called her with the burner phone. As soon as I heard her voice, I lost all the courage that I had spent the entire evening gathering. I dumped the phone on the bed and listened to her.

She kept repeating herself, saying, "Hello, hello, who's there? Who is this? Luke, I swear to God, if you're the person using a strange number to call me, I will kill you. Hello, hello, say something. You know what, I'm blocking this number."

That was when I cleared my throat and said, "Don't block it; it's me."

Silence.

Chapter 13

BRENDA

I was standing at the door when I received the call. I had been so broken the other night when I saw Diana dancing with the woman at the club that I made a mental note to get through each day at the office pretending that we had never met. Day one was not a success, and I had to run home immediately after work because I needed the space and time to properly cry. However, Paxton was not going to let me wallow in peace. As soon as I got home, he was at the door waiting for me.

"Cm'here, darling," he said, and opened up his arms for me to fall in and hug him. Considering all that I had gone through in the last forty-eight hours, I was very much in need of that hug.

"I know you feel like you did something wrong, but you didn't. You did your best to try and save this, and if it is beyond saving, bask in the knowledge that you did your best, okay?" he said.

I nodded and sobbed in his arms. We stayed there for a while, and then he nudged me into the room and said, "I'm going out to get us dinner. I won't be able to stay with you to eat because I have to attend a cocktail party where there will be some film executives. But I would be right back, I promise," he said.

He came back a few minutes later with a big box of pizza for me and said, "Sad people eat calories. Knock yourself out." Then he went away.

It was while I was standing at the door that my phone rang. At first, I didn't want to take the call because why was Luke calling me with a private number? Just as soon as I had made my threat and was about to end the call, I heard her voice. For the first time in days, my world went still.

"Don't block me," she said, and I found myself crumbling to my knees.

"Are you there?" she asked, and I realized that I'd been quiet for a very long time.

"Hi, Diana."

"Hi Brenda, how are you?" she asked.

"I'm okay, how are you?"

"I'm hanging in there," she said. "You?"

"I'm existing."

"You seem like you're having a better time than I," she said.

"What does that mean?"

"I mean, you're getting flowers, and you're having lunch with office boys. I see you around, you know," she said.

"Flowers? What do you mean?"

"Stop, Brenda. I'm not mad at you for trying to move on. This has been hard on both of us," she said.

"Moving on? You're the one who's moving on."

"Shit," she muttered under her breath.

"What is it?"

"I didn't think you were going to see me," she said.

"What did you think?"

"But you're not gay, or at least I don't think you are, seeing as you've moved back to men real fast," she said.

"I'm not sure what you're accusing me of."

"I'm not accusing you of anything. I'm just saying that I see things," she said.

"Things like what?"

"For starters, I saw you receive flowers. I saw you getting in a car with some guy. I also saw you getting to your house with the same guy," she said.

And that was when it finally clicked. All of the times that I had been around Luke as I tried to sort all of this out, Diana had seen us. I immediately started laughing.

"None of this is funny," she exclaimed.

"I know none of it is funny. I'm laughing because I'm relieved."

"Why are you relieved?" she asked me.

"Because I sincerely thought something else was wrong."

"So, this isn't enough for me to be pleased?" she asked.

"I'm just saying that you won't be so pissed when you hear the full story."

"So, what was the full story?" she asked me.

"First of all, the guy you saw me with, the one with the flowers, was like my ex, whom I cannot stand."

"Why are you hanging out with somebody who was blackmailing us?" she asked.

"Because I needed to know what the problem was and what he wanted from us."

"Oh, so you were going out with him because you wanted to know why he was blackmailing us?" she asked.

"I knew why he was blackmailing us. He was blackmailing us because he wanted me back. He didn't want money or anything; he just wanted me," I said.

"Oh," she said, and then went quiet.

"You don't want to hear the rest of the story?"

"Of course, I want to hear the rest of the story," she said.

"So, I started going out with him because I wanted him to delete the pictures and leave you alone. It didn't matter that I hated him; I just didn't want to ruin your life."

"But we were handling it," she said.

"I was already feeling so useless."

"You're not useless," she said. "Most of all, this fight is for you. Yes, I'm fighting for my company, but I'm also fighting for the chance to be with you," she said.

"I know you're fighting for a chance to be with me, but I also want to fight for a chance to be with you."

"And that is okay," she said, "but between both of us, only one person is equipped for this fight, and it's not you."

"Well, it turns out I'm more equipped than you think."

"What do you mean?" she asked me.

"What I mean is that in the process of hanging out with him, I found out what he wanted to do with the pictures."

"What did he want to do with them? Give them to Tommy?" she asked.

"Far from it," I said. "He doesn't even know who Tommy is. He wanted to give them to my parents because my father is a pastor, and my mother is the first lady of a church. They will disown me if they find out that I was dating a woman, and he knows how much family means to me, especially how much I love my mother. He knows it's going to break me if my mother ever found out about me and you that way. He was using her to blackmail me to stay with him."

"So, he doesn't know Tommy?" she asked.

"Tommy is not even on his radar."

"Gosh, I was so jealous," she said.

"Clearly."

"I saw him bring you flowers. I saw both of you coming to the office, and I saw you smiling," she explained.

"On the day he brought the flowers, I went out to have lunch with him and told him that he should do his worst because I no longer wanted to continue with the charade. That was the day I found out that he didn't know who Tommy was and that he had other plans for the pictures. Whatever smile you saw, that was a smile of victory."

"So, he does not know Tommy," she asked.

"Not even the least bit."

"Gosh, I was so jealous," she said.

"Clearly," I said.

"I have missed you so much," she said.

"I have missed you just as much and even more."

"Okay, how about the guy in the office?" she asked.

"Oh, I was reported to HR by my supervisor that I was not paying attention to the data. I was going to be fired. So, I decided to focus on data and do well in the department so that I can be rotated out of it really fast. I had to ask my colleague to help me during break periods so that I could catch up quickly before the next appraisal because HR was very serious."

"Do you want me to talk to her?" she asked me.

"No, please don't do that. She already said that she could not take an evaluation from you because of our relationship. I don't want to cause any more troubles. I'm fine with what is," I said.

"Oh, about the pictures, what did you do?" she asked me.

"I took his phone and deleted them, but he still has the hard copies. Something tells me that he still intends to give them to my parents. To be honest, that is a lesser demon in my opinion."

"Are you sure you want to fight with your parents over me?" she said.

"You look like you're willing to lose your company over me. Why are you currently calling me?"

"I didn't do anything with a woman at the club," she said.

"If you did, it's fine. I'm not going to be mad at you."

"I didn't. We danced, and I kept talking about you the entire time. She got annoyed and decided to have nothing to do with me anymore. Luna is disappointed," she said.

"Well, I'm glad to be the reason for her disappointment once again."

"Tomorrow you're going to meet Luna somewhere near the office, and she's going to hand you a burner phone. We're going to be communicating on that until all of this is sorted out," she said.

***

At the office the next day, I was really chirpy and very intent on working hard. I had read up about data management for the two hours between twilight when I finally got off the call with Diana and dawn when I finally hit the showers. However, that knowledge, coupled with everything that I had been learning in theory and practice, came in handy. My supervisor was very impressed.

"You look like you're finally ready to intern," he said.

"I couldn't have done it without Barry," I said, and then I looked at Barry and said, "Thank you very much."

"You're welcome, Brenda," he said.

"Can I take you to lunch to say thank you?"

"Of course, you can, You're paying," he said.

"It's my treat".

Later that day, while we sat down at lunch, Barry looked at me and said, "Are you going to tell me who broke your heart?"

"What do you mean, who broke my heart?"

"When you started working in our department, you'd go to the restroom in tears and then go to the library and cry some more. You'd come back to the office with your eyes all swollen," he said.

"How are you sure it's a man problem?"

"Because when a woman cries that much, it's often because of a man," he said.

"You couldn't be more wrong."

"So, what made you cry?" he asked.

"It's a private matter, and if you don't mind, I do not want to discuss it."

"Fine, let's talk about our next date," he said.

"Second date?" I asked, confused.

"Yes, second date. Isn't this first one a date?" he asked me.

"This isn't a date. I only invited you out for lunch because I was thankful for the fact that you helped me settle into the department. I'm not interested in starting a relationship with anyone."

"You could just tell me you have a boyfriend, you know. I saw the flowers on your desk," he said.

"If you think every single time a girl gets flowers, the person giving them to her is her boyfriend, then I have a bridge to sell to you."

He looked at me and then went back to his food quietly. The rest of the lunch went by very silently. As soon as we were back in the office, I left and went to the library to get some important documents. Allison came into the library and handed me the burner phone.

"I thought I was supposed to get this from Luna."

"Well, apparently Diana could not wait to talk to you today," she said.

I took the phone and sat, waiting in the library for her call. Three minutes later, the phone began to ring. I picked it up, and I heard her say, "I could not wait to get home so that I could talk to you again. I'm talking to my brother to see if we can find a loophole that we can explore against Tommy."

"Your brother?"

"Yes, I finally told my family about you, but I specifically told my brother the whole truth and how we were working past it."

"Oh, what did he say?"

"He simply said that it was very controversial but that if this was what I wanted, then he was happy for me," she said.

"Oh," I said. "See you later today?"

"Most definitely," she said.

***

When I came out of the library, I went straight to my office to find Barry looking at documents and looking at me befuddled.

"What are you looking at me like that for?"

"Was that why they moved you from Ms. Argon?" he asked, his eyes widened as if he had seen a ghost.

"What are you talking about?"

"Did she prey on you?" he asked me.

"What the fuck are you on about, man?"

He tossed the papers to me along with an envelope. I read the envelope before I scanned the papers, and I saw a note.

I know that I have been the worst, consider this my apology, all my love, Luke. I immediately knew what the content of the package was.

"What the fuck, Barry! How dare you open a package not meant for you!"

"Are you gonna tell me what those are about, or do you want me to go to HR?" he asked.

I had never been that mad at anyone before in my life.

"Fuck off, Barry!"

183

Then our supervisor came in, right in the middle of our squabble.

Chapter 14

DIANA

The next few weeks at the office could have been described as the worst weeks of my life. When the news of the photos surfaced, I was put on suspension by the board because they didn't really know Tommy that well, and they were still deliberating on the votes. They couldn't make him the CEO until they looked into his background. The president of the company had to step up and become the CEO while I was on suspension. The board was afraid of drama and litigation, so Brenda retained her place in the company even though she desperately wanted to leave.

At first, I wanted to blame her for what had happened, but the truth was that it wasn't her fault. It was mine. If I had stuck to the original plan, giving her the phone later in the evening, she would not have left her table to go answer the call at the library. She would have been at her desk when the package came. However, I needed somebody to be angry at, and it couldn't be me, so I transferred all of that aggression I was feeling to her. We argued.

"I'm sorry."

"Sorry isn't enough. How could you be so careless?" I said.

"I was answering the call from you. I didn't even know the package was coming."

"How could you not know that he was going to send it? I thought you said that he told you that he was going to send it to you," I said.

"I knew he was going to send it; I just didn't know when or how. I'm so sorry. I didn't mean to ruin your life. I will leave the company and disappear. I will go back home. I will leave the state if you want me to."

"Do you realize that if you leave the company right now, they will think we forced you to quit? That is such a stupid idea. Please don't offer it again," I said.

"I'm so sorry, Diana. I want to fix this. I don't know how to. Please tell me how to fix it."

"You can fix it by never calling me again," I said, and I hung up on her.

As soon as I hung up, I crawled into my bed, hugged my pillow, and cried really hard. All of this was a mess. I was meeting the disciplinary committee tomorrow, and I didn't know how to feel.

I also refused to see Luna, not because I didn't want to see her face, but because I didn't want to remember that she warned me. However, she was persistent and decided to stay on my patio all night. When I got tired of listening to her sing out loud, I opened the door for her and told her, "You're not allowed into my room." Then I went back upstairs, crawled into bed, and continued crying.

"What was the nature of your relationship with Miss Jenkins?" Mr. Willow asked me at the disciplinary committee.

"We had a sexual relationship of some sort," I said.

"Were both of you involved in a sexual relationship before she joined the company?" he asked.

"Yes, once," I said, but before I could continue, the vice- president of the company interrupted me.

"We didn't ask you to explain yourself, Ms. Argon," she said, shutting me up immediately.

I wanted to explain to them that there were more nuances to this than they thought. I wanted to tell them that I didn't know that she was coming to the company the next morning. I wanted to tell them that all of this was such a big coincidence. But, they were not going to let me speak. The truth was, no matter what my explanation was, there was no winning for me in this situation.

As soon as she walked into the office that day, I had known exactly who she was. I hadn't mention to HR from the very beginning that somebody whom I had just had a relationship with was coming into the company. Instead, I let her come in, and I continued my relationship with her. I had screwed up badly, and it was about to blow up in my face. No, scratch that, it already had.

My brothers left everything they were doing and came down to the office, along with my mother. However, they were not allowed into the disciplinary session. I began to wish that I had done what he had asked earlier and merged my company with Gabriel's. That way, he would have been the head of this committee, and I would have just been a managing director. Yes, I would have been suspended, but I would not have been on the verge of losing my company. Everything was going badly.

"We consider your attachments to Miss Brenda inappropriate and will be placing you on an indefinite suspension until it's time for us to vote," the president said.

I could feel my heart drop. That was what I had feared—the fact that I was going to be on suspension while they were voting. What action said "incompetent" more than earning a suspension? I nodded and said nothing more. I walked out of the office, confused. I didn't know what to do. By the time I came back from my suspension, this company was no longer going to be mine. I had to fight, but I needed to find a vantage point. Right now, I could find none.

From where I was standing, I saw Brenda in front of the data department, her hands clasped. She looked as if she had been through a lot today. I wanted to smile at her, but that was not going to make her life any better. Everybody here was going to think that she was a nobody that I brought into the company, regardless of how well she had performed her assignments. Nobody believed that she was here on merit. While I was destroying my life and all I had worked for, I was ruining her life too. That hurt me more than anything else because she was a young person in the industry, seeking growth. Now I had stolen that from her because I wanted my own satisfaction.

I turned and walked away from her, back into my office where my mother and my brothers were waiting for me. I swear I could feel disappointment in the air as soon as I stepped into that office. Instead my mother looked at me and said, "I know you think they're disappointed in you, but right now we are here to help."

"There's nothing more that you can do, Mom," I said, and I fell into her arms and began to sob.

"Stop sobbing immediately," Dean said.

"What else am I supposed to do? My world has crumbled."

"Not completely," Dean said.

"What do you mean?"

"Before I go any further, there are a few questions I need to ask you," he said.

"What questions?"

"When you branched out of Daddy's empire as he planned, did you change any of the bylaws?" he asked.

"No, I didn't change anything. I thought they were just fine."

"I may have found a way to save you," he said.

I suddenly became very hopeful because if there was anything Dean could do, it was to turn a seemingly impossible situation into a salvageable one.

"According to the bylaws of the company," he began, "the suspension doesn't take place until one week after it has been placed by the disciplinary committee. This grace period was meant to give you time to let the next person into your job seamlessly so that they don't make any mistakes. The idea was that the company runs as smoothly as possible with or without your presence," he finished.

"So, what does this mean?"

He looked at my mother and nudged her on. She looked at me and said, "When your father was starting this company, he borrowed a lot of money from a lot of bad people. By bad people, I'm talking about drug barons, smugglers, black market weapon dealers, and that lot."

"Oh, that cannot be true, Mom," I said, refusing to believe that my spotless father could do something that dirty.

She smiled and said, "You don't know much about your father, but don't worry, it's story time. When he eventually started the company and began to pay them back, they decided that they had found a new way to launder money, refusing to collect the money that they were owed. Instead, they requested shares in the company so that they could launder their dirty money through the company and escape the feds."

I sat down on the floor and crossed my legs, because this one seemed like the story of the decade.

"Your father, not knowing how to fight them, allowed them into the company, but he soon saw that they were intent on taking over the company from him. So, he did something I thought was stupid at the time. As time went on though, I realized that it was a very smart thing to do."

"He went to your uncle and made your uncle sign a document that said that in the event that either he or any of his children were declared mentally incapable of handling the business, your uncle should take over it with entirety. That policy was not restricted by his dying before the children were old enough to understand what the business was about."

"Somehow, he believed that those people were going to attempt to take over the business, so he signed it over to your uncle in the event that none of you were mentally capable of handling the business. He wanted the company to remain in the hands of the family, and whoever it belonged to was going to get it as soon as they were declared mentally capable," my mother continued.

"So, what does it mean for me now?"

She smiled and said, "You have done something that your company thinks is out of character for you. You have been really stressed about work. You are also currently heartbroken…"

I immediately smiled because I understood exactly what she was saying.

"I can see that you're smiling. Here is my phone, Uncle Robbie is expecting your call."

I took her phone from her and smiled; then I called my uncle.

"Hi, Uncle Robbie."

"Hello, Peaches," he replied.

"I need your help, Uncle."

"I was wondering when you were going to call me. I've been hearing about this issue from everybody but you," he said.

"I'm sorry, I didn't know about this safety net until today."

"That isn't a problem. I have been assigned to throw the Hail Mary pass. If you're calling me, it means that you've tried everything else, and nothing seemed to work out. I understand that," he said.

"What do I need to make this possible?"

"Do you have a therapist?" he asked me.

"Yes, I have a therapist."

"Get to the therapist, get the report needed, and get back to me in one week," he said.

"Okay, Uncle," I replied, and the call ended.

"You are the best family any girl could ever wish for," I said as soon as the call ended.

"We know. Also, pack your things; you're coming to Texas," my mom said.

"But, Mom…"

"There will be no *buts*. Your little friend can come too if you want her to," she said.

"She can't come. She's banned from quitting the company, and we can't fire her because we don't want a bad reputation on our hands."

"Are you afraid that she would do something inscrutable?" my mother asked me.

"No, I'm not afraid that she's going to do anything. She cares about me too much, but the company has protocols. I can't break them any further than I already have."

"Fair enough," my mother said. "You also can't see her here in New York, so we're going home."

There was no argument, though I also didn't think Brenda would be willing to talk to me anyway, considering the fact that I laid all of the blame for this on her, even though it was not her fault. So, I went home and packed up, and I left the burner phone on the table along with my own cell phone. I was going to be with my family, and I didn't need my phone with me.

I simply texted Luna with, "I'm going home to be with my family. If you're looking for me, take a flight to Texas. Love you."

I packed my bags and went to meet my family in the private bus they rented. Soon, we were at flying home. As soon as I got home, I went straight up to my room, climbed into my bed, and let the familiar warmth of my sixteen-year-old's bedroom embrace me.

The next morning, my mother woke me up and said we were going to check on a new business venture that she was planning. She took me and my brothers into her car, and we drove down to a wide expanse of land.

"Who owns this land?" I asked as soon as we parked.

"When your father cheated on me, one of the requirements I gave him before I would come back to him was that he was going to let me take the land that his grandfather had left him. Your father was desperate, so he agreed. He did not like it, but then he said that he there was no other person that he trusted more to manage the land, so it was not an issue," my mother said.

"Just how many stories do I not know at this point?" I asked my mother.

"Just the fact that this isn't any ordinary land. The land you see here contains oil," she said.

My brothers and I gasped.

"You see, you're not the only one with secrets. Anyway, I'm going to be selling this land," she said, and then got into the car as if she didn't just drop a bombshell on us.

Chapter 15

BRENDA

It had been four days since Diana left New York and the company without telling me where she was going. I had been trying to reach her on the burner phone and her personal phone without success. It seemed as if she was running away from me and everything else. Someone had mentioned something concerning a set of bylaws that allowed Diana to be CEO for at least one more week. Tommy had clearly not found that copacetic because he was right here in the office, screaming that the bylaws were archaic nonesense, demanding that they be thrown out. He had also demanded that the voting be moved up to the end of this week, and I needed to let Diana know this turn of events. Unfortubately, my call would not ring through her phone line, no matter how many times I tried.

I called Luna and asked her. Initially, she started trying Diana's number too, but then she remembered that

Diana had told her she was going to see her family and had decided to turn off her phone and not talk to anyone while she was with them. I saw absolutely no reason for her to make this decision, and I was really mad that she didn't tell me.

"You look pissed," Allison said to me.

"Yes, I am," I admitted to her. She had come to the office to see me, and we took a walk.

"You know, her leaving without her phones has absolutely nothing to do with you, right?" she said.

"Somehow, I don't believe that."

"You don't have to believe it, but she didn't leave both her phones at home because she was running away from you. She could have just decide not to take your call if that was her intention."

"So, why did she leave her phone behind? Why didn't she tell me that she was going to be with her family?"

"I don't know why she would not give you that information, but I do know that she left her phone behind because she just wanted to rest her head from everything that was going on with her. If she was going to lose the company, maybe she felt that she needed to just do it alone."

"We never do things alone."

"Wake up, Brenda. This isn't a romance novel; this is real life," she said.

"I'm not trivializing the matter. I'm just really upset."

"I understand that you're upset, but you have to let Diana deal with the enormity of this the way Diana needs to. I'm sure she's not trying to lose her company or her relationship, wherever she is. I think she's trying to find solutions, especially given that she's with her family. If you don't trust anything else, trust that at least," she said.

We both stayed silent for a while.

"Do you trust Diana?" she asked me.

"Yes, I trust her."

"Then calm down," she said.

I nodded and said I wanted to go have lunch.

"Lunch is good," she said. "Stop worrying your pretty head. She will be back soon, and you two will sort it all out. I'm positive."

I left her, walked into my office, packed my bags, told my supervisor that I was feeling a little ill. He let me go home. It was Friday anyway. When I got home, I met Paxton in his house and told him the whole story. As soon as I was done talking, he asked, as if it was already figured out, "So, when are we going to Texas?"

I looked at him funny, and then he said, "Honey, if you want to see her, you have to pack your bags and go down to Texas. Stop looking at me like that. Don't worry. I have miles, and I could give you some of them. Just go pack your bags. Let's go to Texas and find your woman," he said.

"But I don't know how to find her when we get to Texas."

"That is a bridge we will have to cross when we eventually get there," he said.

And just like that, we packed our bags and headed for Texas. As we flew to Texas, I couldn't help feeling nervous and looking out the window. Paxton noticed my restlessness and tried to ease my anxiety.

"You know you can't jump, right?" Paxton asked at some point.

"Who says I'm thinking of jumping?"

"You keep looking out the window as though you want to escape. You can't," he said.

"Are you really sure? Why can't I?"

"No, you can't," he asserted.

"What if I go meet the pilot and beg him to turn the plane back?"

Paxton started laughing and said, "Calm down, Chile. What's the worst that could happen?"

"I don't know. What if we get there, and she says that she never asked me to come? What if she asks me to get out of her life and never return? It would be so hurtful and embarrassing."

"I think you're overthinking this. If she says that, we just return to New York and start our lives again," Paxton reassured me.

"You're not starting your life again; that would be just me. I don't think any company would be willing to hire me after leaving my internship in the middle of it."

"Stop overthinking things," he said. "Nothing is ever that bad."

"Maybe this one is that bad. Do you think my old company in Chicago would take me back? I could get back together with Luke; he looks like he has changed. I could..."

"Stop rambling," Paxton interrupted me. "Like I said earlier, nothing is ever that bad. Relax; close your eyes. When we get to Texas, we will go and find Diana, and whatever she has to say, she will say it to your face."

"Okay," I replied and closed my eyes. I wasn't trying to sleep; I just wanted to let the world fade, even if it was just for a few minutes. But, I did fall asleep and didn't wake up until we landed in Texas.

Paxton asked me how tired I was as soon as we landed and remarked on how loud the plane was during landing. I explained that I had managed to sleep through it, but I wasn't sure when I'd had a good sleep last.

"Hopefully, by the time we're done with this trip, you'll have more reasons to sleep," he said.

We called a taxi, and Paxton gave the driver a location. I trusted Paxton's judgment. If he thought we needed to be in this taxi, then we did.

About an hour later, we arrived at a sprawling mansion that looked like something out of a storybook. I was bewildered and asked Paxton why we were there.

"How rich do you think your woman is?" he asked.

"What do you mean?"

"Welcome to the Argon mansion," he said.

I was about to ask how he knew, but he interrupted my thoughts.

"I have my sources, Chile. Quit asking so many questions, and go knock on that door," he instructed.

My heart was in my mouth as I walked toward the giant door. Before I could knock, a well-dressed, middle-aged woman with some gray streaks in her hair came out of the house and smiled at me.

"Hello, young lady, how may we help you?" she asked.

I stammered, "Umm, umm..."

A man who looked like he was in his forties joined her.

"Hello," he said to me without smiling.

I stood in front of these two people, feeling utterly confused, and the words jumbled up in my head. I couldn't find the right words. I just stared at them while they stared at me.

"Oh, for God's sake," Paxton said from behind me and walked up to us.

"Hello, we're here to see Diana," he said.

"Who might you be?" the man asked.

"I'm Paxton, and she's Brenda," Paxton said.

As soon as he said that there was a look of recognition on their faces. The woman smiled more. The man didn't smile, but his expression softened.

"Well, come on in, Brenda, and you too, Paxton," she said.

"I have to go, Mom. See you at dinner," the frowning man said.

"Okay, Gabriel," the woman said, and I watched the man that I now realized was Diana's elder brother walk to his truck and drive off. I concluded that the lady must have been Diana's mother.

"You're not going to stand there forever, are you?" Diana's mother said to me.

"Oh, I'm sorry, ma'am," I said and walked through the door she had held open for me.

As soon as I entered the house, it seemed as though I had walked into a scene from a movie. Not a single thing was out of place, and everything looked beautiful. The curtains ran from a ceiling so high it could have reached from the sky to the ground. Every part of the house seemed like it was brought out of a medieval royal setting.

I knew Diana came from a rich home, but I didn't think it was this rich. What I was staring at was not just riches; it was multi-generational wealth. I could see why Tommy was fighting to get back to the table. There was no kind of personal money that he would ever make that could beat what I was looking at right now.

"Would you like anything?" Diana's mother asked.

"No, thank you."

"Oh, I wasn't asking you, child; I was asking him," she said, pointing at Paxton.

She then pointed at the stairs and said, "That's where you're headed whenever both of you decide to come down for dinner. I'll ask you what you want later. In the meantime, he's my guest, and you are Diana's guest."

I nodded and began to pull my bags towards the stairs. "Oh, no, leave the bags. Someone will bring them up."

I pushed the door open and went inside. There was no one inside. It was like walking into the room of a sixteen-year-old with a very rich father. The bed was a queen-size bed, the walls were painted fuchsia pink, and there were extensive collections of Barbie dolls and stuffed animals on one side of the room. On the other side, there were a lot of books. I must have walked into a time capsule. The bed was neatly arranged, and I was afraid of messing it up, so I found the nearest chair and sat. I sat there, contemplating what to do if she came in. What was I going to say to her? And why did her room feel like it belonged to a child?

I was tired from the flight, so I rested my head on the table and fell asleep. I think I may have been asleep for about thirty minutes before she came into the room. I heard a glass shatter and woke up with a start, staring at her.

"What are you doing here?" she asked me.

Before I could answer, a maid ran into the room and saw the shattered glass on the floor.

"Are you okay, Miss Diana?" the maid asked.

"Yes, yes, Carol, I'm okay. Just come in, and clear it up," she said.

The maid ran out and returned with a brush and dustpan and then began to pick up the shards of glass.

"I came here for two reasons," I finally found my voice. "I came here for you to tell me to go away. That will be the end of this relationship. I will leave New York. I'll go back to Chicago, and you'll never hear from me again. Second, I came to tell you that your brother is in New York, trying to force them to push the vote to this weekend. You need to return if you want to save the company."

"Wait, my brother is back in the states? He was in the UK for a while. When did he return?" she asked me.

"That's a great way to avoid the real matter," I thought.

"Yes, he's back. He's fighting the bylaws that keep you as CEO for the rest of the grace period. If there's something you need to do, you have to do it now," I said.

"What the hell?" she said.

"Believe me, I didn't want to come all the way to Texas to tell you this news. I tried to get Allison to tell you instead. Somehow, she believes that you were here trying to fight for your company and that I didn't need to be worried. I didn't think that's true. I assumed that you were running away," I said.

"No, I'm not running away. I really am here to save my company, but I really needed to rest," she said.

"Did you really mean it when you said you never wanted to hear from me again?"

"Of course, I didn't mean that. I was just mad, and I didn't know who to be angry at," she said. "Unfortunately, you were the easiest target."

"I'm not fodder for your anger," I said.

"I know, and I'm sorry," she said.

At this point, I was just still really mad at her, and I realized that I didn't really want to see her. I looked at her and said, "I have passed the message I came here to pass. There's nothing keeping me here anymore. I'm going back to New York."

"You can't do that," she said.

"My luggage is still downstairs. I'm leaving now. You'll be fine. I can see that you're currently fine. Take care of yourself."

Then I walked out of her room and went downstairs. Paxton was having tea with her mother when I met him downstairs. Another man was with them, and I could immediately tell that he was Dean.

"Thank you so much for letting us into your home, ma'am. We will be leaving now," I said to Diana's mother.

"Oh, Chile," Paxton said and got up.

"You have such a lovely house, ma'am," he said to her, then picked up his bags and continued, "I know a friend around here with whom we could stay. We'll return tomorrow morning."

"Wait, why are you leaving?" her mother asked.

"Honestly, I just came here to pass an important message to Diana and to see that she was fine. I have done both. Again, thank you so much for inviting us into your home. I hope all of this can be resolved. I'm sorry for all the trouble that I may have caused," I said.

"You have caused absolutely no trouble, young lady," Dean said. "I don't know what happened up there, but I didn't think that Diana would be unhappy to see you."

I smiled and said, "I know she's not unhappy to see me, but I can't say that I'm happy to see her right now. Coming here was not a mistake; it just made a lot of things clearer for me. I'll take my leave now. Have a great evening, everybody." I grabbed my bags and left with Paxton running behind me.

As soon as we got into the taxi, he said, "I don't want to know what happened up there because I trust you. If you could see in her face that you didn't want to be there, then you've done your best. Let's go back to New

York; I'm sure we can find something else for you to do. You don't have to go back to Chicago."

"I'm not going back to Chicago," I said.

"Well, good," he replied.

Chapter 16

DIANA

I had never wanted to run after somebody that much in my entire life, but I'd also never seen her that angry at me before. What I saw in her eyes wasn't anger; it was hurt. It felt like I had broken her heart, and I didn't even know how I had done it.

I had not given up on us, or at least I didn't mean to. I could see that's what it felt like when I left the company and New York without telling her, without even giving her a chance to communicate with me. Coming all the way to Texas to tell me that my brother was back and trying to push the vote to the weekend worried me more than the fact that our relationship was about to fail, and I began to feel bad about that.

By the time I finally gathered the courage to come downstairs, she had already left the house.

"What happened?" my mother asked me.

"I screwed up," I said.

"That girl came all the way here to find you, and she left. What did you do?" Dean asked me.

I couldn't defend my actions. "I don't understand. You go through all of this because of her. She came here for you, and you let her leave?" Dean asked. "I feel like you've learned about love from Gabriel and not me," he added.

Just then, Gabriel came into the house and said, "Why are we talking about me and you, Diana? Where is your little girlfriend? I think I saw her somewhere around here."

"She somehow managed to chase the girl away, and that's why I said she was learning about love from you, Gabriel," Dean said.

"Oh, wow! What did you do, Diana?" Gabriel asked me.

"Look, guys, it would be fun to stay here and discuss my stupid love life, but there's a bigger problem," I said.

"What is the problem?" Gabriel asked.

"I need to get a doctor's report from my therapist today. I need to send it to Uncle Robbie today because Tommy is back in New York, and he's trying to move the CEO vote to the weekend while I'm still on suspension and not around," I said.

"What the hell is wrong with that boy?" my mother asked.

"I don't know, Mom, but we need to act fast if I'm going to save my company," I said.

"Get on with the conversation with your therapist now. I'm going to call Uncle Robbie, and we're going to fix all of this right now," Gabriel said.

I ran back upstairs, then realized I didn't have a phone and ran back downstairs. Dean stretched out his phone to me and said, "It was such a stupid idea to come all the way here without your phone. Did you think you were coming to a nature reserve?"

"I know, I know," I said and ran upstairs.

The conversation with my therapist didn't take much time. She quickly prepared her report and sent it to me within the hour. I ran back downstairs and handed over the reports to my mom.

"This will do," she said.

Then, we all entered the car and drove to Uncle Robbie's house. As soon as he saw us, he came out and said, "Never have I seen a mistress cause this much damage in a family. My brother was such an idiot."

"You and I agree on that, Rob," my mother said.

"This is crazy," he said. "Where are the documents I need to sign to take over the company?"

Gabriel handed him a few documents, and he immediately signed them.

"How long do I have to hold on to this?" he asked.

"Not for long, I hope. I'm hoping that this will discourage Tommy from fighting back," I said.

"Hmm," he said and then signed the documents.

"So, when are we going to New York?" he asked.

"On Monday," I said.

"Why can't we go tomorrow?" he asked.

"Because it's the weekend, and the board will not sit until Monday," I explained.

"Are we all here? I think we should all have dinner together," he suggested. "Or have you all had dinner?"

"No, we're about to have dinner when somebody came all the way from New York to tell us in Texas that

Tommy was trying to steal Diana's company," my mother said.

"Who came all the way from New York to pass that information?" Uncle Robbie asked.

"My girlfriend," I said.

"Well, where is she?" he asked.

"She somehow managed to chase the poor girl away," my mother said.

"I see that my brother's genes have somehow found their way into his children," Uncle Robbie joked.

"This DNA is very problematic," my mother added.

Then we all laughed and went to sit at the dinner table. Throughout dinner, I couldn't concentrate. I kept thinking about Brenda and wondering where she was. It was terrible that I couldn't reach out to her because I didn't know how to reach Paxton. But a part of me also didn't want to reach out to her. I knew that I wouldn't be fully devoted to her until I had fixed whatever was wrong with my company. I was on the verge of fixing it, and I hoped that I could fix it really soon because from the look I saw in her eyes, I didn't think she'd be waiting for me when I was done.

"What are you thinking?" Gabriel asked me.

"It has just been a really long month," I said, teary.

"Aww, come here," my mother said, pulling me into a hug. She was seated beside me. "No matter what happens, you have your family. We will always stand by you, and you will not lose this company. Even if it's the last thing we do, we'll fight for it. You worked for this company when you shouldn't have. It has always been your inheritance, but because Tommy was not going to take the one that was meant for him, your father made you work and fight for this company. You won it fair and square, and you're going to own it, okay?"

I nodded.

"Umm, Rob," my mother said, looking at my uncle.

"Yes, Leah?"

"So, remember that land with oil that your brother gave me after he cheated?"

"Yes, I remember the land. What about it?" he said.

"I'm thinking of selling the land, but I don't want to sell it out of the family".

My uncle's eyes lit up immediately.

"I knew that was going to get your attention. Well, do you want to buy the land?"

"I'm sure that I can sell a few of my other properties to own that land. What is your asking price?"

"12 billion," my mother said.

"Paid in full?" he asked.

"God, no. I'm not trying to ruin you."

"Well, how would you like to be paid?" he asked.

"You pay me a certain percentage now. We start work on the land. Then from your profit, you complete the rest of the payment over three years."

"Well, that is a fair price," he said. "May I ask why you're not leaving it to your children instead?"

"Because the oil business is a dirty business, and I don't want my children to ever have to feel that they have to be afraid for their lives because they own something that a bunch of people want. Like your brother, I've made a lot of powerful enemies and a lot of powerful allies."

"I'm sure you'll be fine owning oil land, but my babies will not be. A bunch of people who they don't have the power to fight will come after them, and the truth is that neither you nor I are going to be here long enough to protect them."

Uncle Robbie nodded. He didn't have any children and never wanted to have a family, so naturally, what he owned would be bequeathed to us anyway. He eventually told my mother, when we were not here, that he was going to open the land to mining. He would save the proceeds in a fund that we would be able to access in the event of his death, but he would never have any direct business with the oil land.

***

Monday came, and we all flew out of Texas in Uncle Robbie's jet. The vote of confidence had been done. I had, in fact, been impeached as CEO, and the reins of my company had been handed over to my brother Tommy. They were having a meeting discussing the handover when my family and I walked into the boardroom.

"Good to see you could finally join us," the president said to me. "We have been trying to call you, but you were unreachable."

"Yes, I was in therapy," I said.

"Well, it's a good thing you're getting mental help," Tommy said.

He said that as if it was meant to be a jab. Little did he realize it was his undoing.

I suddenly started laughing and said, "Of course I'm getting mental help. I've been acting so out of character. Which was why I had my therapist declare me mentally unfit to run this company a few days ago."

Tommy looked up at me with questions in his eyes.

"And as of Friday evening, I signed over the control of the company to my uncle here because, before this company was built, the original owner of the entire empire signed a contract with him. They declared that if any of us were deemed mentally incapable of running the company, he would take over until we could finally run it again. Therefore, your vote is null and void."

I didn't have to say much more because everybody in that room knew what this meant. Power had changed hands, and it had happened long before Tommy had a chance to oust me. He couldn't say a word because more than anyone else in that room, besides my family, he knew how powerful Uncle Robbie was. He knew that Uncle Robbie was the one person he could not mess with.

So, he stood up and said, "I resign as CEO."

Uncle Robbie looked at him and said, "We gave you everything. If you wanted to run a company that was under the family name, all you had to do was ask for the one that was given to you in the first place instead of coming here to fight your sister. You were trying to fight your way back into a family you were never kicked out of. Well, consider this an official booting out."

"My brother should have kept you at arm's length, but no, he brought you into the family and made you think that you could fight with your siblings. I never want to set eyes on you again. If I ever do, you'll regret it. And rest assured, your company in the UK isn't safe either. If I wake up on a random day and think that you deserve more punishment for what you've done today, I will come for that company. You know that there is nobody in the world who can stop me when I want something. Now, get out of my establishment."

Tommy nodded and left the room.

Uncle Robbie turned and looked at me, saying, "Just so we're clear, you're still under suspension. Your actions were inappropriate, and they didn't bode well for the company. You could have put us in trouble with the media and our clients. The board will decide what your consequences will be, and until then, the president remains the acting CEO."

He then addressed the president, "Monthly reports should be sent down to me, and I expect you to triple the revenue of this company in the next four months. I don't know how you're going to do that, but I believe that you guys can handle anything. I'll take my leave now."

I kept my face down during the entire conversation, trying to appear contrite. In reality, I just wanted to get out of there and run all the way to that stupid apartment complex to find Brenda. As soon as we got out of the building, I called a cab.

"Where are you going?" my mother asked. "You just saved your company; you should be celebrating."

"Yes, I want to go celebrate," I said. "I'll get back to you."

"You're going to find her, aren't you?" Gabriel asked.

"Yes, I am."

The cab parked, and I got in. The closer I got to her apartment complex, the faster my heart beat. *What if she no longer wanted me?*

When the driver parked, I told him to wait because the last thing I wanted to do was look for another taxi if she rejected me. I went up the stairs, refusing to use the elevator. When I got to her door, I knocked, but there was no answer. After waiting for a few minutes, I knocked again. When I was about to leave, she opened the door, a towel tied across her chest. She moved from the door to let me in. I walked closer and kissed her; then I waited, thinking she was going to be mad.

However, she wasn't angry. Instead, she pulled me in and kissed me. As if on cue, her towel dropped, revealing her naked, wet body. I instantly felt my warmth twitch in admiration of the view. I had indeed missed her.

Printed in Great Britain
by Amazon